I0678534

PEACE ROAD

by

Brad Spencer

ASKME Publishing

Chicago

This book is a work of fiction. The characters and dialogue are fabricated by the author and are not to be construed as real. Some of the events fictionally depicted in this book are based on real incidents.

No part of this book may be used or reproduced in any manner without written permission by the publisher and the author except in the case of brief quotations embodied in critical articles and reviews.

Cover design by Bocheez (bocheez.com). All rights reserved. Used with permission by the author.

Copyright C. 2016 by Brad Spencer (BradSpencer.net)

All rights reserved.

ISBN 13: 978-0692722091

ISBN 10: 0692722092

ASKME Publishing, Chicago

Also by Brad Spencer

The Upshot

A note from the author

The summer of 2015 was one of the most violent on record in Chicago. There were 36 gunshot victims during the Fourth of July weekend alone, including 21 in an 11-hour stretch. The month of August yielded an average of more than 40 shootings per weekend. In September, the city was hit with 59 murders and 362 gunshot victims, including two consecutive weekends during which more than 50 people were shot.

Most of the shootings were gang related.

With at least 75 gangs and more than 600 gang factions, Chicago had been labeled the gang capital of the U.S. The city had become a hub for the Mexican drug cartel and its associates who distributed mostly heroin and cocaine across the country.

During this time, the country was reeling from racial tensions in the wake of the death of an unarmed African American by a white law enforcement officer. Chicago and its police department would soon be the epicenter of its own controversial officer-related killing, also resulting in an investigation by the U.S. Department of Justice.

Peace Road is a work of fiction but much of it is based on actual events. I wrote it with the hope that someday Chicago would not be home to such rampant violence and racial unrest.

I hope that time is now.

Brad Spencer

"I believe that unarmed truth and unconditional love will have the final word in reality. This is why right, temporarily defeated, is stronger than evil triumphant."

— Martin Luther King, Jr.

"Being against evil doesn't make you good. Tonight I was against it and then I was evil myself. I could feel it coming just like a tide... I just want to destroy them. But when you start taking pleasure in it you are awfully close to the thing you're fighting."

— Ernest Hemingway, Islands in the Stream

END OF THE ROAD

Autumn

Is Harry West alive?

THE MICHIGAN FOG hung thick in the pine forest as sharp rays of the first morning's light sliced through open space.

The car rolled up to a blockade of thick tree limbs that had been placed across the dirt road. Beyond the roadblock, the flanks of the dirt road were littered with junk of the rusted out metal and steel sort, scattered amongst the high growth of grass and weeds. A rusted barrel, surrounded by white corroded metal chairs and stacked crates, smoldered near a whitewash trailer.

Empty beer cans were strewn about the area around the barrel.

Forty or so yards beyond the whitewash trailer was another trailer, this one larger, corroded in lime green and connected to a cedar porch anchored by cinder blocks used as steps. A window was covered with a black plastic trash bag and duct tape. A torn screen door swayed from one hinge on a light breeze. An old beat-up Camaro was parked next to the trailer.

At the blockade of tree limbs, Lyndi Carnes cut the engine of her cruiser. She studied the terrain.

Moving the tree limbs would be a task and driving up the dirt road would for sure warn the occupants in the trailers, she thought. Walking up the road made more sense, catch them by surprise.

But should I call the local authorities, get some unis out here? Dumb question LC, now get your ass up to that first trailer.

She went to the back of the cruiser, raised the trunk up, slipped off her shoulder holster and slipped on a bulletproof vest. She grabbed a pump-action shotgun and made sure it was fully loaded before leaning it against the back of the cruiser. She took her Glock 19 from its holster and switched off the safety, then stuck it in her waistband. She took the two reserve magazines on the holster and shoved them in her pockets. She put her hair back in a ponytail and fitted her dark blue police ballcap onto her head.

A deep breath before picking up the shotgun.

I will bring them in or I will kill them here.

After a firm rack of the shotgun, Lyndi heard the sound of a car slowly trundling up the dirt road behind her. Turning, she leveled the shotgun at the windshield and gripped the trigger gauge firmly, waiting for the vehicle to round a sharp bend. The car, make and model irrelevant to her, emerged from the fog and stopped. The driver's door opened. Lyndi pointed the shotgun at the driver and braced herself for the recoil of the blast. He stepped out slowly, almost methodically as if the effort was difficult. When he stood, Lyndi recognized the leathery grin first and lowered the gun. The passenger stepped out of the car, not looking at Lyndi but scanning the area, maneuvering his head around the thicket of foliage for a better look up the road to the trailers. He wore a bullet proof vest and a holstered handgun on his right thigh. He stood in a crouched position, peering through the foliage.

The two men looked haggard.

Jebediah Hatch, the driver, spoke first. "Mr. Flisk and I decided to go for a drive and take in the majesty of autumn's colors."

Lyndi flashed a hard smile and nodded. She took a few steps toward them and spoke in a hushed tone. "Not sure what kind of hell's waiting up there."

She turned to Dave Flisk and tossed him the shotgun. He was ready for it, snagging it with one hand. "Slip through the woods there on the right, get as close to the edge where the trees and weeds meet and find some cover," said Lyndi. "Start blasting if you see anyone draw a bead on me." She turned back to Jebediah. "You bring your piece?"

He nodded and pulled his Kimber 1911.

"Creep up high on the left flank, stay at least twenty, twenty-five yards away from me in the likelihood they have assault rifles."

He nodded and made his way through the foliage. Flisk was already gone.

Lyndi drew her Glock from her belt and started up the dirt road, pinning the gun back behind her right thigh out of view of the trailers as to not provoke an all-out gunfight too early. If that happened, they needed to be closer to have any chance at getting out alive.

She slowed her breathing to keep the puffs of white breath from clouding her line of sight. The damp cold air reached through to her bones and she stiffened up to the point where she was clawing her boots through the clay-like mud of the road. She reached the corner of the first trailer, stopped and crouched, listening to anything other than the crickets and the tree frogs. She had made it this far without anyone seeing her.

They must be asleep. Or gone.
They're neither, Lyndi.

She nodded to Flisk that she was heading up to the second trailer. As she reached the cinder blocks used as steps to the porch, she could see a hazy film of fog hovering over a mossy pond just off to the right of the trailer. For some reason it made her think of her father, the two of them fishing somewhere long ago, baiting hooks and catching blue gill.

Lake Geneva.

She briefly wondered what he was doing at that particular moment, watching her from heaven, shooting his way out of a shit storm in some far off country, sleeping off a hangover in a hammock in the Philippines. She wondered if he ever thought about what she was doing at a particular moment.

The pond also reminded her of the place Harry had taken her just a few months back. It was hidden behind a farmhouse. It was the last time …

The thought quickly vanished when she heard a raucous coming from the trailer. Someone was foraging around for something.

Could be someone retrieving a weapon.

4

She raised the Glock at the door—a piece of plywood nailed over what was once a window.

"Hey dog, yer gonna make me some breakfast! Now get up!"

The man's voice was loud and gruff. Lyndi heard the squeal and muffled cries of a woman. It sounded as if she was being smacked around. She sidled over to the door and leaned against the trailer.

"No! You're gonna keep your clothes off until I tellyas to put'em on! Now fry me up some eggs!"

Lyndi reached for the door handle, but before gripping it she heard a man's voice from behind.

"Whatya think yer doin?"

She turned.

He was gaunt and dirty, wore a faded denim jacket with the sleeves cut off, ripped up jeans and old work boots. A withering cigarette burned in his lips, a near empty bottle of Corona dangled from two fingers in one hand.

"Leroy don't like early visitors. But yer welcome to come down to that there trailer and wait. We can find something-somethin nasty to do to one another." He grinned and teetered back a bit.

Lyndi figured he was drunk or looped up on something. But either way, he wasn't speaking loud enough for the occupants of the trailer to hear.

Grabbing his crotch, he growled, "I'll let you play with my snake."

"Sure," said Lyndi quietly, pointing the Glock at his chest, "but first do me a favor and raise your hands up."

"You like playing with guns, too," he said. "Well, this is gonna be fun." He raised his hands in the air—spilling what was left of the beer—his body listing and his eyes narrowing.

"How many boys up here like to party?" asked Lyndi, moving closer to the man, stepping lightly across the rickety cedar planks of the porch.

"Part, party? Well, hail, we all like to party, especially with a fine woman like yerself. Yeah, we'll take turns on you, sister. You'll get it good and hard from all of us, and, Leroy there, he'll even get Fat Annie to part-partis, partis-pate. So c'mon, come on over here now," he grabbed his crotch again, "give daddy a mouthful."

"Tell me something first," said Lyndi. "Is Harry West alive?"

The man looked surprised. Dropping and then raising his arms up in unison, he shouted, "Hail, no! Leroy done killed that neg—"

Three quick successive shots, one atop the other, their bluntness nearly making one sound. Two to the center of the man's chest, one to the center of his forehead. He was dead before his body hit the ground.

Lyndi didn't have time to admonish herself for the poor decision. The trailer door blew open, she ducked and side-stepped, searching for cover.

A magnificent blast.

Sharp pain on the right side of her body—hip, torso and shoulder burning.

Pellets, Lyndi, keep moving. You're not dead. Training. Slow your adrenaline. Breathe. Breathe.

She stumbled to the side of the trailer as a large half-naked man wrapped in muscle and ink kicked open what was left of the door. He was forced off the porch by a high blast from Flisk at the tree line that scattered chunks of siding into the grass.

Flisk was running toward the trailer now, racking the shotgun, his face twisted in anger, revealing desperation for the missed opportunity.

Lyndi yelled, "No, stay back!"

A few men scattered out of the far trailer, shirtless, stumbling, all pointing weapons, rifles, handguns, running up the road toward the trailer by the pond, firing wildly at Flisk. He took two rounds—one a straight-through shot to his left calf and another a graze to the back of his neck—before he went down and crawled behind a rusted out snowplow blade.

The men kept at it. Bullets pinged off the metal of the blade, blew up the weeds and dirt to his left and right, and ripped through the leaves of foliage behind him. He tried to return fire but the onslaught forced him back beneath the cover of the blade, crumbs of rusted metal spitting at his face.

Leaning against the trailer and trying desperately to control her breathing in an effort to ease the pain of her wounds and keep her wits, Lyndi knew she could not run or hide. She took in a painful breath and edged around the corner, popping off two shots at the man on the porch before spinning back and out of sight.

She turned to move around to the other side of the trailer but was stopped by a chainsaw hanging upside down on a laundry line, flies buzzing around it. It appeared to have bloodstains across the blade and dried flesh hanging from the chain. Lyndi blinked it away and focused on what to do next.

"Get me the Bushmaster, dog!" she heard a man holler from inside the trailer.

She willed herself up and around the corner, smearing blood across the grime of the siding. She made her way up to the blown-apart door, and went in.

*****

7

Jebediah Hatch couldn't watch the fusillade of bullets ripping around Flisk any longer. He was parallel to the police officer but in the heavy foliage to Flisk's right, back past the last trailer. He had seen Lyndi Carnes go into the trailer in pursuit of someone. Men were shooting at Flisk, who was pinned down behind a snowblade. And Lyndi had appeared to be in bad shape when she stammered into the trailer.

There's no time for overthinkin things, Jebediah.

*****

Flisk buried his head in his hands and clinched his eyelids shut tightly. He tried hard to picture April and Daniella in a happy moment. April holding the baby and smiling in the backyard of the new house. Her smile still looking a bit forced but with a hint of sincerity. She had whispered something to him, out of earshot of the FBI agent who had been assigned to their case. Flisk had leaned in closer. She said, "I'll go anywhere with you."

It was her mantra ever since the trouble in Fenton. It was meant to inspire him to move on, to let him know she'd never give up on him. She believed in him. The three of them would start anew somewhere else, if that's what needed to be done.

I'll go anywhere with you.

It made him forget about the bullets ripping up the snowblade in front of him, whizzing past his ears. It made him forget the pain pulsating in his neck and calf.

Then, in an instant, the chaotic barrage of bullets ripping into metal and earth dimmed, and Flisk could only hear the loud pops from a nearby handgun. He felt the blood on his neck trickle down his back warmly as he turned his head upward. He blinked away the dirt, the sweat, the tears and saw the old man standing there in the open, stiffly firing his weapon, a cold glare to his face.

"Get down, old man!" Yelled Flisk.

"I got no reason to," replied Jebediah as the bullet strafing picked up again. He continued to fire, changing out clips by digging into his trouser pockets for more. Flisk heard the faint cries of pain from beyond the snowblade. He looked up again to see Jebediah gone.

Is he sprawled out in the thicket of weeds?

"You hit, old man?" he called out.

When there was no reply, Flisk snuck a look over the snowblade. He could only see the back of Jebediah moving away from him. The man was headed into the fray, still stiffly firing, bullets whizzing past him. It sounded as if he was roaring like a lion, taking a breath and then roaring again. He seemed to turn and shoot at one man until he was satisfied they knew he was coming, then turn at another and do the same.

The sight of the old man stalking into the deadly gauntlet jolted Flisk from his abandon. He pushed himself up and racked the shotgun.

The roar and the blast.

Firing, racking, roaring, Flisk limped hurriedly to the old man's side. Together they moved down the dirt road, side-by-side, firing away. When the shells were used up in the shotgun, Flisk tossed it aside and drew his Beretta and kept up the barrage.

ON THE ROAD

CHAPTER ONE

Summer

Just to be remembered

FROM WHERE HE leaned against his car on a quiet overpass near Garfield Park in Chicago, Harry West could see the men, women and children filing out of the funeral home and gathering near a black and silver hearse parked out front. They mostly wore dark colors but no one was really dressed up for the occasion. Most of the men paced about, peering up and down the street.

They looked on edge, paranoid, thought Harry. Or, just waiting for someone or something to set them off. Or they were eager to go downtown for the protest.

My expectations may be too high for that.

Hundreds of people stood out front of the brick building. Some of the females were in slinky dresses and high heels. An older female mingled among the group, fanning herself with a folded up piece of paper to try to keep cool from the heat. Children ran about in the parking lot, oblivious to where they were and why they were there.

A tall, thin and bald man stood out from the group, his pale white skin and his white cassock conspicuous among the throng of African-American family members and friends of the deceased. He seemed to be walking around to each man, placing a hand on a shoulder and bowing his head.

From the overpass, Harry had a birds-eye view of the congregation. It wasn't much to behold, nothing like the funeral held for a police officer awhile back, he recalled. Dignitaries from far and wide came to that funeral. A mile-long procession, complete with newly washed squad cars with their blue and red lights flashing. White chairs in thirty rows of ten. A cascade of flowers making a horseshoe shape around the chairs. One massive bouquet adorned with an enlarged photograph of the officer in uniform. Bagpipers and all.

Harry checked his phone. He had to be in court soon. He didn't want to miss the protest, but duty called.

Just then a dark blue cruiser pulled up alongside his car. He grinned and nodded at the tinted windows.

Lyndi Carnes got out of the cruiser carrying a paper bag, damp at its bottom. The two didn't greet one another. She went right over to his side and leaned against the car, opening the bag.

"I picked up a half dozen artery cloggers off Hubbard. You want one?"

"They soak those doughnuts in grease for about six hours, LC," he replied.

"Best pastries around," she said.

"How do you keep such a gorgeous figure eating like that?" he asked.

"Oh, Harry, sometimes you need to indulge in the most sensual pleasures, no matter how harmful, sinful or … fattening." She wrapped up the bag and tossed it on the hood of his car. "Speaking of sensual pleasures, you busy tonight?" She brushed her brunette hair from her forehead and smiled at him.

Harry noticed a group of younger men make its way to the parking lot where they were soon drinking from bottles and smoking what looked to be marijuana joints. Some of the men took off their formal shirts and were wearing tank tops. A few men donned skullcaps, black and white. A bass beat from a car thumped through the air.

He shook his head. "It's sad really," he said, now staring off over the rooftops of the neighborhood, "an eight-year-old girl laid to rest last year and only a handful of people at her burial. But here, this guy …"

"The vic who was caught in the gang crossfire?"

"Yeah, only a few family members and me," Harry looked down and pinched the bridge of his nose, trying to hold back a rush of emotion.

"You went to her funeral, Harry?"

"Yep." He sighed. "Yes, I did."

"You didn't tell me that."

"These guys don't give a shit about trying to prevent the violence. They don't give a shit about changing the culture. They could be going downtown right now to peacefully protest the killing of their friend, their brother.

But instead they're drinking forties in brown paper bags and smokin dope in the open."

Lyndi looked back out over the crowd. "All he had to do was put the damn knife down when the officer told him to, Harry, and he'd still be alive and they'd just be doing this somewhere else when on a break from selling heroin to rich suburban kids and trying to blow holes into their rivals."

"It's not as easy as that, LC," said Harry in a shallow voice, his eyes transfixed on the group below. "You wouldn't understand."

"Why, because I'm not black? Or is it because I'm a cop?" She didn't wait for him to answer. "The kid, Jaylen Roy, was on PCP, Harry. Who knows what he would have done."

"Yeah, maybe he was too high to realize what the hell he was doing, but he didn't deserve to be shot full of holes in the street." Harry's face turned more serious. "You know, the kid, he was a client of mine once. Kept him from doing a three-to-five stretch for selling smack near a school. First-offense back then."

"He should have wised up then," quipped Lyndi. "You play with fire—"

"But, LC, you think that cop would have shot him fifteen times for holding a knife if he were white?"

She shook her head. "Doesn't matter what I think, Harry. It's about the training. It's about protocol. If there's a threat of bodily harm you empty your service weapon until you feel the threat is neutralized." She folded her arms at her chest and looked up at him. "I'm not going to get into a black and white debate with you." When he didn't look her way she asked, "What's with you? What are we doing here?"

"You do this job long enough it can grate on you. He was a pretty messed up kid, and this is a pretty messed up situation. Most of them are. No fathers. No one who cares. No chance." Harry took a deep breath. "And whether you want to believe it or not, your colleagues have gotten away with some pretty nasty things in this city."

"My colleagues? They are also your colleagues, Harry. It's public service work. We just get paid from diff—I don't want to argue about this with you again." Lyndi put up her hand.

"Corruption from the top-down," said Harry. "Chicago's known for it. From the days of Capone to Jon Burge and his cattle prod. You know, I read an article that stated in the last ten years the city has doled out more than five hundred and twenty million dollars in alleged police misconduct cases?"

"Jesus, Harry. What are you trying to start here?"

"Settlements, Lyndi. They were paying out settlements."

"I'm leaving, Harry." She began to walk away from the car.

"I'm sorry. I don't know why I'm being an asshole."

She stopped and turned around. "It's a pretty messed up world. Not putting down a knife when several officers are telling you to–"

"I know, LC, maybe it would have happened some other way but whose fault is it? Society needs to do more to help kids like him. These other guys," Harry pointed down to the crowd, "the older ones who somehow survive another day, they're not going to change. But the young guys, the guys in their preteens. They have a chance."

Lyndi shrugged and moved back closer to him. "Sometimes nothing can be done. Maybe the officer saved an innocent kid by taking out a known gangbanger high on PCP," she paused, looking intently at him. "You seem to be carrying around a lot of guilt lately. Something on your mind?"

"No, nothing." He sighed again. "I'm just caught up in all the tragedy, I guess." He stood up off the car. "This gangland warfare that's raging, racial tensions on the rise, political corruption ... Chicago just isn't a civilized city. It's turning more and more a dystopia. A shit show. And I just can't seem to wrap my head around any answers."

They stood in silence for a moment before Lyndi said, "Well, we're in the business of serving. This is as good a place as any for that." She stood up off the car, turning toward him, her face looking eager to change the subject. "So, how do you want to go out, Harry?"

He was put off by the question. Once again Lyndi Carnes showed no emotion to the tragedies going on in her city. A cold-hearted homicide detective, loyal to her brethren in blue. She didn't understand the travails of a poor black kid from the inner city. But, man, was she beautiful, fun and smart. And he loved her, even though he had no idea if she felt the same way.

Harry hesitated, watching the group in the parking lot grow by the numbers.

"Just to be remembered," he finally said. "That's all I ask. That someone remembers that I tried to make a difference." He adjusted his tie and quickly wiped moisture from the corner of his left eye. "I'm due in court but I will take you up on that offer tonight."

Lyndi smiled at him. "Alright," she gently poked her finger into his chest, "but leave the sulking and the sorrow and all the antagonizing bullshit at the office."

He nodded.

As they were both getting into their vehicles—Harry scooping up the paper bag from his car's hood and stuffing a mouthful of doughnut into his mouth—Lyndi said, "It's going to be okay, Harry."

With Chicago's skyscrapers rising off in the distance on the clear day, he watched her drive off.

"I'm not so sure, LC," he said to himself.

*****

"Pulled any riot duty ever, Flisk?"

No answer, just a wipe of a thin layer of sweat from his finely trimmed beard.

"Flisk?"

He turned, annoyed. "What?"

"You ever work one of these riots?"

"It's not a riot. It's a protest," answered Flisk. "No, nothing this large, just little sit-ins. No rank and file stuff."

The big guy to Flisk's right shrugged. "Well, the more the merrier. Gives me a reason to let off a little steam and bash some heads in. Jesus, don't these people have jobs?"

"Shut up, Boggs." Flisk turned away from his partner, peering at the enormous group of protesters chanting and wielding placards outside City Hall. He turned and looked down the line of police officers standing as barricades to keep the protesters at bay.

"Hey, you know I heard the guy that shot the kid has a hot young wife. I may have to try to tap—"

"Fuck off, would you?"

"What the hell's up your ass? You got a girl, Flisk?"

Flisk nodded hoping he would shut up.

"Married?"

He nodded again.

"Shit, the whole time you've been workin for CPD you aint ever mentioned you had a wife. You're a quiet motherfucker, you know that? You got kids?"

Flisk rolled his eyes, and adjusted his helmet. He was starting to sweat profusely now with all the gear on. "One, a baby girl."

"You know you ought to get that chip off your shoulder, Flisk. We're supposed to be your friends. You want us to have your back."

"It's a chaotic time for cops in this city right now, Boggs. Sorry if I'm not Mr. Social at work."

"Jesus, you aint ever been Mr. Social. You're Mr. Socially Inept. You're also one moody sonuvabitch, you know that? I'm here in this getup on my day off and I gotta listen to your shit? My day off!"

Flisk only looked up at him, his upper lip slightly quivering. He was aggravated by the ignorance of his partner. Boggs stood there, his big six-foot-six frame towering over the other officers in formation. With his reflective gold-tinted sunglasses and his childlike grin, he looked like an asshole. Flisk considered punching the jackass right there but thought better of it.

Man, wouldn't that make the five o'clock news.

"There's not a thing I would do for these bottom feeders of society," grumbled Boggs.

"Shut-up, man," Flisk said harshly.

"Fuck you, Flisk," retorted Boggs, while looking over at the officer to his right and gesturing a do-you-believe-this-guy look. He turned back toward Flisk. "You starting to feel for those gangbangers, now, too, Flisk? Where'd you say you came from anyway? St. Louis? Man, that's nothin compared to the scum up here. You need to get that straight. You've been in the jungle now long enough to know that."

As the chanting quelled, a solemn silence fell over the protest. Then the group marched onto LaSalle Street and suddenly bodies went down one-by-one.

Flisk was amazed at the solidarity of it all. Hundreds of people of all ethnicities lowering themselves to the hot pavement. Heads rested on the body parts of total strangers, and no one objected. When the cabs and the cars finally stopped honking and the rattle of the elevated train faded in the distance, the scene was eerie but profound to Flisk.

"That's unity, right there," he said. "A community of one." A sense of envy came over him. He hadn't seen such solidarity in years.

Not since before the …

"Yeah, well, let's go crack some skulls," hollered Boggs as their unit commander directed them to forcefully remove the protesters from the street.

*****

Jebediah Hatch was in his 2003 Chevy Malibu inching his way in traffic, trying to get back to his home on the near west side after reluctantly spending two days down in Bridgeport with his daughter and his grandkids. It was nice seeing the family, but he was anxious to get back to his neighborhood. He didn't like Bridgeport with its commercial, entertainment, and arts infrastructure. But then again he didn't really like his neighborhood either, only for different reasons.

Traffic was now at a standstill. After switching on the radio, Jebediah realized what he had driven into.

He began to think about the kid and the officer. He was relieved it wasn't in Back of the Yards. There had been enough bloodshed of late with all the gang wars going on. More than usual.

They shot that kid up for nothin, thought Jebediah. He wanted to say it out loud to somebody.

Shot him up, left him in the street. No witnesses, but them. For nothin. Same thing that happened down south awhile back. Shot an innocent black kid in an alley. White cop got off on that one. Whole world going to hell in a handbasket. Who can be trusted? Gangs ruling the streets. Black versus white, hasn't changed, just evolved.

"Whole world going to hell in a handbasket, I say." This time Jebediah said it out loud and felt a little shameful. An old man stuck in traffic, the heat of summer thick in the air, windows down, talking to himself in his car. This is what he'd become. Grumpy old man. Curmudgeon.

He changed the subject in his mind.

I don't know why she won't keep at least a lil pea shooter in the house for her and the kids.

"'Bridgeport not like that, daddy.' Shoot, everyplace got lunatics anymore. And aint nobody gonna keep me from protecting myself and my house and home."

Jebediah looked around. Nobody was listening. Every car in his vicinity had its windows up, no doubt the occupants enjoying the cool air-conditioning of their vehicles while stuck in traffic. He just waved his hand. "Whole world going to hell in a handbasket, I say."

CHAPTER TWO

My name is Harry West

MY NAME IS Harry Joseph West. My age: 42. Birthdate: May 2, 1972. Social security number: 355-87-5554. Driver's license number: S155-0548-3542. I was born in a small town in Illinois called Elburn to Joseph and Beatrice (Betty) West, both deceased. I went to the University of Illinois and received my law degree from Northwestern University. No wife or children and no siblings.

I worked as a public defender in Cook County's Felony Trial Division for seventeen years. When I started off I was excellent at my profession, mostly as it related to securing unexpected and exceptional plea deals for my clients. I was a good persuader and negotiator, and I was passionate about my principles. I wanted to see the system work as it was intended. I wanted to see those accused of committing violent crimes receive their due process of law. I wanted to see those incarcerated for committing violent crimes become rehabilitated and sent back out to the real world to live lawful and productive lives.

I never got to see any of that.

I saw ignorant clients decline no-jail plea deals entirely out of loyalty to their gang brethren or because serving time aided their authoritative reputations. I saw clients go to prison for short stretches only to get released and commit more crimes. I saw killers that I poured my heart and soul into defending go free only to kill again.

Ruthless criminals who served minimal sentences for their crimes because of my intrepidness got out of prison and ended up killing innocent children and adults—mothers, fathers, sisters and brothers.

Sure, I helped save a few people. Some who served brief time for their crimes got out and got jobs, settled down, had a family and lived conventional lives. But, overall, I indirectly had a hand in killing too many innocent lives.

It's a burden unbearable.

My name is Harry West. If you're reading this, then I am dead.

-HJW

CHAPTER THREE

I go by Lyndi, Lyndi Carnes

THEY SAT ON the end of workout benches in-between their sets, looking at their biceps and then at her, and then back at their biceps. They seemed to engage in an internal struggle with themselves on what deserved more attention, their own muscles or the beautiful woman working out.

Some were a little less obvious, stealing glances as they looked up at a television hanging on the wall, ESPN replaying Sportscenter for the hundredth time. They'd stretch, look up, look at her, and start the cycle over again while pretending to wait for the availability of a certain elliptical machine.

Some checked her out for her taut and firm body, the result of good genes, usually good eating habits, but mostly good workout regiments. Most men were entranced by this attractive woman's focused and determined intensity, especially when it came to her chin-ups.

The motion was smooth, her breathing synchronized with the rhythm. Although her arms were likely burning, she held a concentrated look of pleasure in her face. They could picture laying beneath her in bed. The up and down motion, the sweat, the light brown hair pulled back in a ponytail, the mildly freckled ivory face, the muffled moan, the furtive grin.

It was difficult to look away.

Lyndi Carnes paid no mind to the ogling. The chin-ups were always near the end of her workouts. By now her tank-top was usually fully soaked through, her skin glistening with sweat. She'd grab a towel, swipe it across her brow, dab her chest, wrap it around her neck and trot to the showers, leaving the feverish stares in her wake.

Being attractive wasn't something she relished, more an added bonus. Being tough, staying tough both physically and mentally was more her nature. Both her parents served in the Army, mom as an intelligence officer, dad in Special Forces, where he still may or may not be a member of Delta Force, a counterterrorism unit in the secretive Joint Special Operations Command. Jack Carnes lived and worked defending CIA annexes all around the world.

Jack and Sherry's divorce when Lyndi was young did little to cause angst in their only child. But her father's disappearance when she was eighteen was another story. The two had been close. They had spent a lot of time together when Jack wasn't off on a mission. He taught her weapons, how to use and how to identify them. Handguns, machine guns, shotguns, rifles. He also taught his daughter self-defense techniques, including a mix of martial arts that consisted of Filipino Kali and Jeet Kune Do.

By the time she was seventeen and the star quarterback on the high school football team wanted more than just some kisses and a cop of her breasts, Lyndi was a master at self-defense. His hand went down her pants and the thumb, index finger and pinky were broken with her thighs. She held back the urge to dislocate the shoulder of his throwing arm in the process. "I won't say 'no' twice next time," she told him. When he sneered at her, she added, "Or, 'no' at all."

None of the men she dated ever lived up to the memory of her father, a tall, fit, rugged man who always spoke with a crackling authoritative voice. He had a brash military disposition that never wavered even around his daughter.

While strolling out of the locker room one afternoon nearly a year or so ago, freshly showered and adorned in her dark, slim pantsuit, Lyndi had recognized Harry West. He wasn't like the buff jocks at the gym in their spandex shorts and their muscle tees kissing their biceps and adjusting their crotches, or the young power-happy male cops she worked with who were short in stature and always scowling like bulldogs. He wasn't like the other attorneys she had come across, usually married and/or arrogant, not to mention profoundly out of shape.

Harry West was thin, svelte, light on his feet. Being herself a basketball fan and a former high school and collegiate player, Lyndi quickly sized him up as a lean Blake Griffin. When he strolled through the lobby of the fitness center he had done so with a masculine elegance, a confident poise. He had a thin dark head of hair, eyes blue, and faint mocha skin. She figured him to be Latino or a racial mix. Exotic nonetheless.

She was impressed that he had looked at her without molesting her with his eyes. "Lyndsey? Lyndsey Carnes?"

"I go by Lyndi, Lyndi Carnes," she had corrected sternly, while employing a firm handshake. Every time she said her own name there was another faint remembrance of her father, who designated the nickname "Lyndi" and combined the short version of her middle name, Suzanne. She had to remind herself every time, she was no longer Lyndi Sue.

"Yeah, you took batting practice on Freddy The Stooge Gant," Harry West had recalled.

It was way back when she was a patrol officer. She had testified against Gant, who had attempted to rob a jewelry store in broad daylight, beating the owner with a baseball bat. Lyndi had rolled up on the beating in progress. She wasn't able to prevent Gant from getting off a few pops on the jewelry store owner but she made him pay just the same. She had approached Gant from behind as he raised the Louisville Slugger and kicked him square in the testicles with her thick, department-issued shoes. She then swiped the bat from his grip and took a cut at the back of his kneecaps for good measure. This was back when cops weren't being filmed relentlessly during every arrest attempt or had to wear a body camera.

During the brief trial, Harry tried to make it sound as if officer Carnes had used excessive force, but it was difficult to do with Freddy The Stooge Gant being three hundred-plus pounds and this young beautiful female cop on the stand.

"I swung at a low cutter." She had smiled when she had said it. Harry was older. She always flirted with older men, something she assumed had to do with her relationship with her father.

"Yeah, I was glad you admitted to it. Most cops wouldn't. Integrity. But a lot of good it did me, right?" Harry had replied. They shared a short chuckle. "You know I believe The Stooge is still walking funny."

They enjoyed another brief laugh.

"So, how you been?" Asked Harry.

That's how it had begun. That's how the beautiful but tough Chicago cop and the sincere but complex public defender came to be together. That's how Lyndi Carnes stumbled upon yet another satisfying but likely short-term romance. She never allowed for any man to stick around too long. It was her life. She'd live it how she wanted. She had no plans to ever be a wife or a mother. Men were meant to be temporary in her life, a quick fix for companionship, sex, adventure.

But Harry West was different. Even after a little more than a year, she had yet to cut him loose. But she would, she always reminded herself of that.

Love just wasn't her thing.

CHAPTER FOUR

I have a life to die

"DURING THE VICTIM impact statements, the defendant, Mr. Delgado, was called, among many things, evil. But it was Socrates who once said that the only good is knowledge, and the only evil is ignorance.

"Mr. Delgado may be a lot of things, but a certain set of unsettling circumstances can lead to a person's immoral behavior.

"The only good is knowledge and the only evil is ignorance.

"Your honor, Raymond Angel Delgado is not evil in the sense he's been portrayed in this court room. He is a man who was raised in foster homes throughout his young life. His mother emigrated from Mexico to the U.S. in search of a better life for her children only to end up a crack addict. She eventually overdosed. The only thing Mr. Delgado knows about his father is that his dead body was found floating in a ravine in Guanajuato, Mexico with a bullet in the head. Mr. Delgado was abandoned before reaching the fifth grade, the highest level of his formal education.

"These DCFS reports I hold in my hand, your honor, state that between the ages of ten and thirteen Raymond Angel Delgado was repeatedly physically abused by family and non-family members, virtually homeless, and thrown into a life where he had to learn how to survive on the streets.

"And that's exactly what Mr. Delgado has done, your honor, survived. Because it's all he's ever known.

"Raymond Angel Delgado is a man who had the deck stacked against him from birth. He reached out for help but our system, as it exists, is not equipped to give people like him help.

"Raymond Angel Delgado is not evil. Surviving is not evil. The only evil is ignorance. Raymond Angel Delgado never had the opportunity to better himself with knowledge. He was too busy surviving.

"Your honor, a wise man once said, and I quote: 'I plead for a time when we can learn by reason and judgement and understanding and faith that all life is worth saving, and that mercy is the highest attribute of man.'

"With that, sir, we hope that you find it in your heart to sentence Mr. Delgado to the minimum requirement for these charges. We recommend treatment for Mr. Delgado's own drug addiction under the TASC statute and that you graciously take in Mr. Delgado's serious health concerns when deciding upon his sentence."

"What was it, a heart murmur?" growled the judge.

"Yes, your honor, a congenital heart murmur. Thank you."

Harry West sat down, pleased with his performance. He hoped it would make up for the no-show of testimonials for his client's character and his client's pathetic opportunity at allocution. "I don't know," Delgado had said. "I'm sorry, I guess?"

That's what Delgado had said. That's all. Of course, against his defense attorney's advice.

Would it kill you to show compassion? Harry had thought as gasps and angry mumblings filled the courtroom following his client's brief speech.

The public defender adjusted his tie and felt a twinge of pain again behind his right ear. He had awoken that morning with yet another severe headache, the third in a row this week, probably the twentieth in the last three months. The trial had weighed heavily on him. Delgado's arresting officer, a Sergeant Dave Flisk from the Gang Enforcement Unit, had sat in the front row directly behind him staring daggers for the entire trial. The first couple of days of this was enough for Harry to do an intensive background check on the officer, see if there was some sort of vendetta Flisk had against his client. Arresting officers don't usually stick around for trials before or after they testify. He uncovered no such thing, but did find out something personal about the officer.

One afternoon during a break in the proceedings, and while Harry was yet again nearly incapacitated with another one of these massive headaches, he let the information about the officer spill to his client. It was an unprofessional misstep, Harry knew, and he regretted it the minute he had said it. The guilt and the shame continued to consume him.

He reached for a glass on the table, trying desperately to grip it tightly, but watching it slide through his fingers. He took the glass with his other hand and softly put it back down.

The pain behind his ear grew stronger with each breath, so he slowed his breathing. He gripped the glass again, this time with two hands, and brought it to his mouth. It probably looked odd, a grown man taking a drink from a glass with two hands, but he did it anyway. Closing his eyes, he took long gulps of the water, then tried to savor the taste in his mouth.

There's no taste to water anyway, he told himself before changing the subject in his mind.

We could ride the bikes along the lakefront, kayak the river. Maybe she'll take a trip somewhere with me, sometime soon—it would have to be soon—like the west coast or maybe somewhere nice like Puerto Rico, wipe the savings account clean. We could rent a boat, frolic on the beach, maybe swim with stingrays, go parasailing. She'd love all that. I could tell her everything. Maybe not. It never seems to be the right time.

It for sure wasn't the right time on that overpass watching the mourners drink and smoke and act like damn fools, when they could have been downtown trying to make an impact with their presence and their voices.

Harry waited for the judge to stand and dismiss himself, to adjourn the sentencing hearing so he could retire to his chambers and contemplate his decision, a routine procedure. But the starchy, gray-haired judge simply put on his reading glasses, moved a manila folder from one side of his bench to the other, licked his lips, and looked up.

Oh good, thought Harry, let's get this over with. *I have a life to die.*

"Mr. West, once again you have done an excellent job defending your client—and your speech for this trial was … well, eloquent but only somewhat comprehensible and persuasive. Was that indeed Clarence Darrow, the famed defender of lost causes, you referenced?"

"Um, yes, your honor. From Leo—."

"Leopold and Loeb. I'm aware of the case, counselor."

Uh-oh.

The judge's voice went from warm and soft to cold and crisp. "I believe EVIL, the force in nature that gives rise to immoral conduct of character, most certainly does exist, and it's sitting right next to you in the form of Mr. Raymond A. Delgado."

The pain behind Harry's ear continued to throb. A thin sheet of sweat formed on his brow and he felt the undeniable urge to use the restroom. A succession of twinges popped off in his head. He imagined wires in his brain beginning to short out, or ripping through his skull like a current of electricity.

The meds are supposed to numb this?

Harry West was a Cook County public defender in the Felony Trial Division. Which meant he provided counsel for some of the most ruthless criminals. It had been seventeen long years since his first case, defending a lunatic named Leroy Crump. It was quite a learning experience. Crump, being a self-proclaimed racist and Harry having a black mother and a white father, wasn't the ideal first client.

"I AM a black man!" Though it was obvious, Harry had felt the need to announce this to his client after Crump had rambled on about how blacks were a disgraceful race. "The one DEFENDING YOU!"

"Only when you want to be," Crump had replied, laughing sinisterly, his shaved head protruding out in a ball of milky pastiness from his orange jail-issued jumpsuit. "Now get on yer mule and get me a deal. Chop-chop, times a wasting."

Harry's skills as a litigator had come a long way since his first client. He proved to be an excellent attorney, a distinction that only grew stronger with each case. He became well respected in the profession, not just from his fellow colleagues, but from the friends, business associates and family members of his clients. He was the free lawyer who could get you off on murder or any tight felony rap. Public defenders from other divisions came to him for advice, like what to ask for in a complex plea deal, who to call to the stand, or how to circumnavigate the legal system. Harry knew it all. He had a stable of admirers, from clients, colleagues, prosecutors and judges.

And it certainly wasn't like he did any of it for the money. The salary was pathetic. He lived modestly in a bungalow on the near north side of Chicago. His lawyer friends were making big money in private practice, driving fancy sports cars, living in the posh suburbs in large homes. They had cabins and ski boats on pristine lakes up in Wisconsin, Michigan, down in Key West, Florida. They wore expensive suits and were members of country clubs.

Harry chose this particular legal work because he wanted to make a difference.

He blinked his eyes a few times—a thin blurriness subsiding—wiped his moist hands over his face, and scratched the back of his head. Shocked, he sat staring at the starchy old judge.

Did he really just say that?

His client, Raymond Angel Delgado, was standing, hooting and hollering, hugging family members and high-fiving his friends amid gasps from the other side of the courtroom. The judge was pounding on the gavel, trying to restore order.

For the first time in his illustrious career as a public defender, Harry sat in a courtroom uncomfortable, dumbfounded and utterly jaded.

A suspended sentence?

"As I was saying before I was interrupted," barked the judge, "despite Mr. Delgado's penchant for indiscriminate behavior, I'm asserting a suspended sentence of forty eight months on the Class three felony conviction because I feel incarceration would only continue to inflame the evil in his soul.

"If Mr. Delgado fails to adhere to the terms of his intensive probation which will include being monitored to find legal and gainful employment and stay away from gang activities, he will face the maximum penalty of five years in prison.

"Mr. West, I highly suggest you explain to your client the consequences of any future unlawful actions he may participate in. He doesn't seem to be listening to a word I'm saying. Neither do you for that matter.

"Mr. West? Mr. West? MR. WEST!"

That's when Harry's mind went blank and he blacked out.

CHAPTER FIVE

Fate is a fickle jade

"THAT FOR WHICH we fight is to safeguard the existence of our race, the pur … pur … ity of our blood and the sus-ten-Ance of our children."

Bill Holland stepped in for a closer look. He could smell the man's foul body odor from a few feet away. There were small beads of sweat forming on the man's massive back. Holland read the tattoo again, this time louder, this time more confident.

"That for which we fight is to safeguard the existence of our race, the … purity of our blood and the … sustenance of our children."

He was able to get it read again before the man's back convulsed inward and then dropped out of sight, only to retract again and appear in his vision line.

The statement or declaration or whatever it may have been was stenciled in dark green ink and flanked by large swastikas. The man's arms were painted as well, from his neck on down. When the man turned around to face Bill Holland it was a collage of Swastikas, 666s, shamrocks, swords, eagles, skulls, Sig runes, theatrical masks—some ablaze in deranged smiles, some drowning in sinister expressions, and a cornucopia of interlocking triangles across his chest, arms and neck. There looked to be a spider web tattooed across the man's shorn head.

As Holland continued to study the man's skin curiously he made out the letters, PW, and the words "Heil Hitler" and "Mein Kampf." He took a deep swallow and finally looked into the man's eyes.

"Name's Leroy Crump," said the man, taking one giant step out of the hole. "Nice to meet you."

"Uh, hi. I'm William, Bill, Bill Holland. You a friend of Ms. Deets?" Holland shook the man's big burly hand nervously. Once Leroy Crump's dark flinty eyes connected with his, Holland felt the need to look downward and scrape his shoe along the dirt.

"Fat Annie is my wife," said this Leroy Crump, somewhat of a young man, probably in his thirties, who stood at least six-foot-five and probably weighed, Holland estimated, two hundred and twenty pounds. He was a wall of muscle in skin, dirty jeans, and work boots.

"I let the fat-ass bitch marry me while I was down doing time in Marion. I aint got but that old Camaro to my name, but I'll likely sell it. Find me some decent wheels."

"Nah, I don't need no Camaro," answered Holland, only glancing upward, not realizing this Crump wasn't offering to sell the car to him. "They'd likely repo it if they got word I had one of them. I live off disability checks from the government. These trailers here, and ole Jake, is all I have, all I need." He pointed to a trailer down the dirt road about a hundred yards away. It had a porch off the side with a table, chairs and a bright yellow umbrella. It butted up to a mossy pond that had a short pier made of wood. Holland looked around the yard for the dog, perplexed.

"Oh, good for you, Bill, suckin off the tit of the government. Nothin says freedom like takin money from those lepers in Washington, er, wherever the capitol of Michigan is or wherever the hells they at. Am I right?"

Bill Holland nodded but he didn't know why. It just felt like that's what he was supposed to do. "You hunt, Bill?" asked Crump.

Holland nodded again.

"You got some shotguns, rifles, maybe even some handguns?"

"I do."

"Good! How's about semi-automatic A-sault rifles?" Crump had leaned the shovel against his chest and made quote signs with his fingers as he said the word "assault."

"I have an assortment of hunting rifles and handguns for my own personal recreational use, yes. Why do you ask?"

"No reason, just curious."

"What you diggin a hole fer, mister Crump?"

Crump smiled. "Why does any man dig a hole, Bill, if not to put something in it?" He resumed stabbing the shovel into the dirt and stomping on it, shaving off the edges to make it wider. It was already five or so feet deep.

"What you aimin to put—"

"So Bill, how'd you hurt yourself?"

"Say what now?"

"How'd you come about gettin checks from the government, livin for free in that there double-wide trailer with the cedar porch attached?"

"Oh, I slipped on a wet spot in a Piggly Wiggly over in Antioch a long while back. Hurt my lower back. Somethin like the third and fourth lumbar vertebrae—hail, I don't know, but it's kept me from havin to work. I spent twenty-two years at that Piggly Wiggly, going up and down ladders, carrying all sorts of heavy boxes and what not. Then, one day, just slipped on a wet spot in the aisle. Boom. Laid up for weeks. Can't hardly bend over anymore. Can't run. Never did really run anyways. Can't lift anything over my head like-this." Bill Holland raised his arms up over his head.

Leroy Crump stopped digging. He speared the blade into the dirt and then walked around the pit to where Bill was standing. "You build that there cedar porch yourself, Bill?"

Standing chest high to Leroy Crump is all, Bill quivered as the tattoos became more prominent. *Kill'em All.* It was in italics right across the front of Crump's throat.

"Fat Annie tells me you don't have no family," said Crump. "And she say she's the only friend you got. So, who built that cedar porch?"

"Well, I got a dog named Jake round here somewheres, and, well, I built that porch ah-course. It wasn't all that hard. I just—"

"Where you keep the deed for yer trailer, Bill?"

"Now you listen up. I don't like the way you're speakin to me. I rent that there trailer to Fat Annie—I mean to Ms. Annie Deets—and I have rules that have to be followed here. This is my land and that's my trailer and this is my dirt and people just can't go round diggin holes in my land. Strangers, strangers just can't go round diggin holes in my land. And … and … and I rented that there trailer to … Annie and nobodys else. So as far as I'm concerned, you need to leave until-until Annie comes back and straightens all this out for me."

Crump took a step closer. A bead of sweat rolled down his forehead, and then his nose, dripping off the tip and landing on Bill Holland's boot. "Tell me Bill, how's that fat ass bitch been payin the rent?"

"She gets a subsidy or somethin, lives off food stamps," Bill muttered. "I aint sure. She pays every month. She good about it."

"Just because I'm a convict don't make me stupid, Bill. I did a lot of reading during my stint. Now, stop wasting my time and get in the hole."

The command flustered Bill Holland. The shiver started in his head and poured down into his feet. His knees spoke a rattle, and he couldn't slow his breathing. There were guns, of course, in the trailer far back behind him, and Jake.

Where the hell was that damn Rottweiler?

"I killed your dog, Bill. I aint sorry bout that. Sometimes I get these episodes where I just fly into a rage and want to tear the hell out of anything. Yer dog reminded me of a lazy ass ape at Marion that my brothers and I didn't get a chance to stick a shiv into."

"I aint that," said Bill softly, the pleading in his heavy breathing. "I aint nothin but a man who rented a trailer to a woman named Annie Deets."

"I know, Bill. Fate is a fickle jade. Now, I killed yer old dog. I aint sorry bout that. But I am sorry bout—"

He needed just one hand to grip Bill's throat. He didn't need to grab the entire neck, just the Adam's apple. He dug his fingers into the tendons and the muscles around it, before seizing his hand into a clinched fist, the cartilage crackling. Bill fought as best he could, slapping with his arms, sidling with his rubbery legs. But Crump had instantly crushed Bill's hyoid bone. Bill's legs gave way and he crumpled to the ground, Crump keeping his grip all the way down, leaning all his weight into the hold as Bill's head hit the dirt. Crump then used the pressure of his weight and the ground to snuff the rest of Bill Holland's life from him.

"—killin you, Bill," Crump said before dragging the body by the pantlegs into the pit, atop the dead dog.

*****

His father taught Crump the creed: "That for which we fight is to safeguard the existence of our race, the purity of our blood and the sustenance of our children."

The Crumps believed that all other races were inferior to the white race.

Leroy Crump believed so much that at twelve years old he shaved his head. At sixteen years old he got a small tattoo of a swastika on the right side of his neck. Two years later he was so angry at the government and its greed, he decided to rob and beat the first government employee he came into contact with. He went stalking the streets on his way to the county courthouse, but he never made it there.

Leroy robbed and beat a U.S. Postal Service mailman. The mailman wasn't exactly considered a government employee—not since the early 1970s—but Crump hadn't been aware. The mailman was African-American, so in his mind it was two-birds, he figured, with one fist.

Leroy wasn't too keen on his court appointed attorney, a young man named Harry West, fresh on the job for the Cook County Public Defender's Felony Trial Division. But Leroy briefly relented his burgeoning hatred for the inferior races when West organized a plea deal with the state's attorney. Off the table was attempted murder as a hate crime. On the table, due to no priors, was aggravated battery and armed robbery. Deal. Still, Leroy refused to shake his attorney's hand, which seemed to suit Harry West fine.

Off to Marion Prison in rural southern Illinois, Leroy Crump went, serving seventeen of a twenty-five year sentence. Twenty hours per day alone in an eight-by-seven room surrounded by concrete.

But Crump took the opportunity to expand his mind, his ideals, to strengthen his convictions, find religion, and do his best to keep such fresh influences secret from the parole board.

While at Marion he became an ardent devotee of the Prison Ministry of the Church of Jesus Christ Christian.

Leroy Crump became a member of the Aryan Nation.

He had always been a sociopath.

CHAPTER SIX

My cover has never been compromised

IT WAS A dark office, the blinds half drawn, allowing only a slit of sunlight. As his new boss concluded his formal introduction, Dave Flisk could still hear the dull drone of the bustle from the morning rush on the street below.

"Officer Flisk, I've told you a little about myself. Now, let's talk about you."

"Sure. It's Dave, sir, David Flisk," he fidgeted nervously. "I've been with the Gang Enforcement Unit for more than a year now and I'm learning a lot. I've got a good idea of all the players from the leaders on down to the runners to the lookouts. I know the symbols, the gestures, the codes. I know the gang territories, the girlfriends, the users, the dealers. I've cultivated numerous informants.

"As you can see in the file there, my arrest record has been excellent. And I'm hoping to some day gain enough experience, skills and knowledge to move up in the ranks here and eventually make my way to the Drug Enforcement Agency."

The long silent pause concerned Flisk.

"Officer Flisk, as you know, as your new commanding officer, I have been briefed on the confidential circumstances pertaining to your background and how you came to the Chicago Police Department. I am obligated to notify you that I have been briefed of this. And to be honest, I'm really baffled that your former commanding officer, knowing what I know now, permitted your request to join the Gang Enforcement Unit in the first place."

He cocked his head and scowled. "Why's that, sir?"

"Well, nothing to do with the incident that took place in Fenton, but in regard to your safety and the safety of your fellow officers."

Flisk sat up a little straighter. "My cover has never been compromised, sir. And there's no correlation between what took place back then and my duty enforcing the law as a part of this unit."

The commander put up his hands and leaned back in his chair. "Officer, I don't want you to think this is a black and white thing. I may be an African-American man—I'm a veteran cop and, trust me, I know the job. But I always keep the safety of those under my charge and this city's citizens as my number one priority.

"You've done well the past year in this unit, that's not up for debate. But the stakes are different now. What we have right now in this city is a cauldron steaming and it's going to boil over." He counted off with his fingers. "The mayor fired the super, the chief administrator of the Independent Police Review Authority resigned, the chief of detectives up and quit, and all of us are taking additional roles here ahead of a god-damned Justice Department investigation.

"Now, are you sure, with what you've been through, that I can trust that you'll continue to serve without prejudice?"

Flisk only returned the commander's stern expression.

"What you do on your off time is your concern," said the commander, "but I won't have you trying to intimidate those you've collared in court while you're supposed to be on duty. Do I make myself clear?"

Flisk nodded.

"I just want to make sure," continued the commander, "you're not driven by other forces other than your obligation to the department and to the people of Chicago."

"I'm sorry, sir, but what are you referring to?" He watched as the commander exhaled an exasperated breath.

"Perhaps your own personal ideologies? It would jeopardize the safety of the entire unit."

Flisk nearly rose from his chair, putting his hands stiffly on the arm rails. His face turned red. "My conduct has never been detrimental to the unit or the people of Chicago, sir." His lips tightened. "I am not a racist. I don't collar these gangbangers because of the color of their skin or anything other than the fact they've committed a crime. I didn't kill that kid," he forced himself to say his name, "Marcus Johnson, because he was black. He was killed because ..." He wiped his face, trying to change course in his wording. "Look, the Missouri State Police and the United States attorney gen—"

"Listen, Dave, I know you've been put through the ringer for sure, by internal affairs, the media, the general public, and yes the attorney general. I don't care about them. I'm here in front of you now. I run a tip-top unit with little patience for indiscretion of any kind. And with us being put under the microscope, it's a no-tolerance policy with me whatsoever.

"I'm keeping you on this unit, but I'm also keeping an eye on you. I need you physically and mentally fit. So, I, personally, need to find out that …" The commander looked down at his file, peering through his bifocals on the tip of his nose, "Dale Fisher," and then his eyes darted back up, "is not in this unit, but David Flisk is."

I've done nothing to warrant being told how to conduct myself! I thought this interview was a get to know you, see how close I was to getting promoted before all this shit went down.

"Do I make myself clear, officer?"

My past has nothing to do with my job performance. Fuck you, you piece of—

"Officer?"

"Yes, sir."

CHAPTER SEVEN

I hope that boy comes back

A GROUP OF young men and women sat outside in the tall grass behind an old dilapidated house, the roof with a dirty tarp over a portion of it, a window or two boarded up, a shiny black Mustang parked in front.

"This here is Mikey Coughlin, the dude I told you about. He play ball for Naperville North. Southpaw, vicious fastball and knee-bucklin curve. He makes dudes look stupid at the plate. My man here is going to Notre Dame to play ball! And then, who knows, on to the show! Right, Mikey?"

Mikey, in a T-shirt and jeans, grinned, then flexed a bicep and looked at it lovingly. Someone handed him a beer.

Another man, sitting cross legged on the ground, his face full of patches of scruff and baby like features—a small nose and mouth—looked up. "Yeah, the white boy you said is loaded and drive a new Mustang. This is the kid?"

"You know it. Kid can play some hoops, too! We was hoopin down on twenty-third and Lawrence, and my man Mikey was killin it from long-range!"

Mikey glanced at his bicep again.

"You a terrible basketball player, Bolt! You can't even get up and down the court without wheezin!" said the man sitting on the ground.

"I'm a role player, man. I screen and crash. Not like you, Skugs, you don't give up the rock. And you can't hit the broadside of your own fat momma with it neither. Now, do me a solid and set my friend Mikey up. He want the H, and he got himself some pins and he got himself a roll."

"Yo, Bolt, what dope I got, I done used, man. Last night Teresa and I went for a ride. It was beautiful, man."

Mikey Coughlin took a swig from his beer bottle while peering around the backyard. It was nothing compared to his backyard in Naperville. There wasn't a waterfall cascade through a mound of boulders that fed into a large, salt-water pool, a putting green, or a tennis court. "What's your name, chief?" He asked the little guy sitting on the ground.

"Hey, kid, aint no stranger ask nobody's name round here. Okay? Names aren't important in this hood. You can call me Skugs."

"Well, Skugs, I got a roll of hundred dollar bills and I want to chase the dragon. So can you set me up or not?"

Everyone seemed to stop what they were doing, whether it was talking, smoking weed, or drinking, and looked up. Skugs scrunched up his tiny face with curiosity. "You white, rich suburban kids are all the same, man.

You don't know when to flash and when not to." Skugs stood up. "You drive in, kid?"

"Yep," answered Bolt, a tall, gangly young man with slouchy shoulders, a narrow head and caverns under his eyes. He was nodding his head enthusiastically.

"Yeah," said Mikey, briefly adoring his bicep again, "I brought the five-point coyote in. Why?"

Bolt pleaded. "C'mon, Skugs, stop messin with him and give him—us—a taste."

"I told you, dumbass. I aint got any and if I did, I wouldn't be sellin it to yall. Teresa'd kill me. She loves the stuff. I gotta scratch some coin together for our next trip."

"Here's a twenty, Skugs," said Mikey, ripping the bill from his roll of cash, "just point me to who you buy from."

Skugs looked at him, perplexed. "I don't know, man. Them boys get nervous when new blood come round."

Mikey ripped three more twenties from his roll and tossed them on the ground next to Skugs. Two other people jumped at the cash, so Mikey peeled off three more and tossed them down. Soon, others at the party were leaping for the money.

Skugs began to contemplate, raising a finger to his chin in thought. "Well, you can go to Laramie and get Tar from a Black Disciple. Though the Two Sixers are sellin some mean Mexican Mud down on fourteenth."

He went silent for a moment, his finger tapping his chin. And then his eyes widened. "I know what you need, white boy. You need a Whiz Bang and Night Train's crew has got nasty Whiz Bang. You got to go over near Seventieth Place in West Englewood for that. You'll see them on the corners. Ask for a guy named Pablo. He set you up."

Bolt turned to go, excited.

"No, you stay," said Mikey. "I'll go hook us up and bring us all back some. Make this a real party."

As Mikey walked out through the house, Skugs looked at Bolt. "That white boy, alright," he said.

"Sure is," answered Bolt, a smile stretching his face. "He gonna set us all up!"

Suddenly, Skugs looked bewildered. "Say, Bolt? That white boy gonna drive that fancy Mustang into Imperial Gangsta land?"

"Ah, man, he a big boy. He'll be fine," Bolt waved him off and began talking to a woman.

"In West Englewood? I hope that boy comes back."

CHAPTER EIGHT

Stay frosty

THE LAST TIME she saw him was the summer before she went off to college. They had done some kick-box sparring in the backyard when Jack received a phone call. He left for "work" abruptly that evening and never returned. His last words to Lyndi were, "Stay frosty." It was his signature sign-off.

There have been moments throughout her life that she has felt his presence. During a basketball game in college when she was bringing the ball up court, she thought she had seen his face in the stands. But after the game there was no one in the seat. While on her way to the Chicago Police Academy graduation ceremony she thought she had spotted a man following her to the Blue Line train. He entered the same car at the far end, but by the time she made it past the riders and down to that side of the car, a stop had come up and the man was gone.

And then there was the time when she found a torn piece of paper with a phone number on it in the pocket of her police jacket while patrolling a beat. Under the number it read, "If you need to. SF."

At first, she figured it was just from another bozo who was hitting on her, playing some stupid mind game. But when she considered the possibility that SF could stand for "Stay frosty," it set her off.

What, he doesn't have the balls to face me? Well, I don't need to and I won't ever NEED to.

Lyndi had spent her young life trying to impress her father, to win him over. Whether it was in sports or school work or listening intently to his instructions, she sought out his approval. She rarely succeeded. As she got older, his absence angered her more and more. She vowed never to call the number, under any circumstances. She memorized it and used it as a symbol of motivation for whatever obstacles ever got in her way.

Her mother, who knew the nature of her husband's work and its consequences, never tried nor had the desire to find out if Jack Carnes was still alive. His missions were classified and his whereabouts unknown. She filed for divorce a year or so after he didn't come back from a mission and went on with her life, eventually marrying a commercial real estate investor. They lived in south Florida until her death a few years ago. Lyndi and her mother had never been close. Except for the occasional exchange of Christmas cards, they had rarely kept in contact. Lyndi figured her mother had a new family and a new life, and that Lyndi would only be a memory of Jack Carnes.

After college, Lyndi went to the police academy—which was a joke in her eyes—and then to work as a patrol officer for the Chicago Police Department. She did seven years in uniform and another four as a line squad detective before arriving in homicide. She was now a veteran homicide detective in the Area Central Division. And she planned on being a commander someday.

CHAPTER NINE

There is only so much worth having

"*MUJERES HERMOSO*. AS many as you can find," said Raymond Delgado to his bodyguard, Tiny. He wanted to celebrate with a bevy of beautiful *senoras*. "*Un grande fiesta! Mucha comida y bebida.*"

Delgado was in a good mood. He had dodged jail time. Not that there was an inclination that he wouldn't. Delgado felt nothing could ever truly cage him, not his enemies, not the law, not the courts, not even a woman. Not even the beautiful Alexa Rojas, sister to his friend and partner in crime, Edgar Rojas. She had been coming on strong lately, urging him to stick to just one *amante*, one lover. Alexa insisted that she, alone, could keep him happy. She was beautiful, but she was also wild. And that wild side always had Delgado thinking she was just as cunning as her older brother.

Edgar was a born salesman. Also hailing from Guanajuato, Mexico, like Delgado, he had made some key connections. He was on his way to lieutenant status in a much bigger organization than the Latin Kings. Shipments had been made. With the help of Delgado's gang, things were in place for a lot more product to flow through Chicago. More high level dealers were being lined up. The low-level corner dealers were already a dime a dozen. The network was about to explode and make Delgado and Rojas extremely rich and feared men.

"Tiny, is Edgar back from Mexico yet?"

"No boss, *mañana.*

"When he gets in, tell him to bring his fine lookin sister to the party—and all of her friends."

"Alexa?"

"*Si*, Alexa."

"Oh, Alexa, a fine *puta*, boss. Heavy on top. Long stems. Sweet behind."

Even though the man was twice as big and three times as muscular, Delgado glared at the man he called Tiny. "Have you and Alexa—"

"No, boss," Tiny cut him off. "Never. None of us have ever tried. She only want the boss."

Delgado looked at him curiously, searching his face for a hint of doubt. "Keep it that way," he said before dismissing him with a wave of his hand.

He sat back in his chair and once again contemplated whether or not this relationship with the cartel was a stupid risk or the jackpot to wealth and glory. Edgar had spoken about the fancy cars, the mansions, the opportunity to go anywhere they wanted in the world any time they wanted.

"A silver jet take you clear across the world, Raymond," Edgar had said. "You'll be able to buy anything you want."

Delgado had demurred, "There is only so much worth having, Edgar."

"We, *amigo*, will soon have it all." Edgar had said it with great expectations bursting from his eyes.

But Delgado remained skeptical. He knew he was already playing with fire. Any slip and he'd be doing a lengthy stint in prison. But Edgar had assured him that they were in bed with the right organization.

"We cannot fail, *amigo*," he had said. "They can own everyone. I have sold them on our status here and on our prowess. They think we control Chicago. And soon we will."

But it was still a huge risk that worried Delgado. It was like Alexa. She wanted to control him, keep him only for herself. But if he said no, that he was going to keep his cadre of ladies, then she'd eventually lose interest and take up with some other *hombre*. He didn't want that.

Delgado did not want to be beholden to the ruthless cartel and he did not want to be beholden to the beautiful Alexa.

But a man can't always quell life's temptations.

CHAPTER TEN

Six months, maybe

SHE STOOD OVER him, her long brown hair pulled back in a ponytail and hanging down over her left shoulder. The overhead light caused a glare off the badge clipped to her belt.

"Harry, why was I not allowed in here until right now? They said it was your choice to keep me in the waiting room."

"I didn't want you to see me like this."

"So, what's the diagnosis here? What have the docs told you?"

"Oh, they think … they're for sure it was just an anxiety attack or something. I've had a lot on my mind lately. Chock it up to stress. Not enough protein in my diet."

"It's more than that, Harry."

Harry tried to organize his thoughts. The meds were making him groggy. "What are you talking about? I passed out, no big deal."

"From what the bailiffs said you had some sort of episode?" She waited for a response but didn't get one.

"Episode?" He finally asked.

Lyndi folded her arms up over her chest. Sighing deeply, she said, "A seizure, perhaps? I don't know, Harry, you tell me. The docs won't tell me anything, claiming privacy laws."

Harry smiled. "If you were my wife they'd tell you everything you wanted to know." When she didn't react, he continued, "I passed out, LC, probably hit my head on something. I'll be fine. Hey, do you want to take a trip somewhere?"

"No. What? Yeah, you did, Harry, you passed out, after you started convulsing in your chair, foaming at the mouth and pissing yourself, you passed out. It was a seizure, wasn't it?"

"No. They say it was more an extreme panic attack from too much stress and not eating right, that's all. I'm fine, honest. But did I really piss myself?"

She raised her eyebrows. "You don't have to tell me, Harry. I'm not your wife and I'm not your girlfriend."

"I know, LC. You're nobody's girlfriend. But what are you? What is this?"

"I'm just your friend who happens to be a woman. This is what I call friendship."

Harry groaned. "You're a good friend, LC. So I was thinking maybe San Diego or Puerto Rico, or what about Hawaii? Do you have some time-off coming?"

When she didn't reply again, he slowly put his right hand back and propped up his head. He looked up at the ceiling and began to contemplate something. "You know, the vic I was talking about this morning, the little eight-year-old girl? She was sleeping over at a friend's house when a stray bullet went through the wall, caught her in the ear." Harry peered into the shadows of the room for a moment. He turned back, tears welling up in his eyes. "Thirty-seven bullets, LC."

"I know, Harry, I was on the scene shortly after. Tragic." She shook her head, but her eyes remained dry.

"Thirty-seven bullets and not one, not one, hit their intended target," said Harry. He wiped his eyes clean, but more tears filled the space. "One traveled more than a hundred yards, went through a wall and into a child's head. Just a little girl who was hanging out inside a home with her friend. And like that," he tried to snap his fingers but they didn't meet, "her life was over. The light snuffed out. She was given just eight years in this world. Some of us get … Hell, if the damn bangers just killed each other off it might be a safer city. Just give them a place to rumble, free of innocent people."

Harry tried to halt the tears. He sensed Lyndi was aware of the effort. He watched her ease off her gruffness by leaning into him and stroking his forehead. "Hey, it's gonna be okay," she said. Her scent would always get to him, something like roses and pink grapefruit. He tried desperately to rekindle the smell.

"I've got to get back to work," she said.

He peered at the freckles on her face, wondering if she knew a man this close wouldn't think of her as so tough. "My job," he said. "I think I'm going to step away from it for a while. I need a break."

She looked at him bewildered. "Listen, I know I'm odd about the relationship thing but I do care, just don't know how to express it is all. Anyway, I want you back and healthy, like the way you were. You'll get there," she patted the white sheet next to his arm. "They'll discharge you soon and I'll stop over in a day or two after a shift." She kissed him on the cheek and started for the door.

"Lyndi Carnes," he called out.

"Yeah, Harry?" She turned.

"We'd make some great babies."

She smiled weakly before turning and walking out the door.

*****

Earlier, Harry had listened attentively to his doctors inform him that this seizure was likely the first of many to come. He was advised to take time off from his work, get his personal life in order.

In order?

The doctors also informed him that at this point a procedure involving a partial craniotomy and a partial resection of his temporal lobe to try to keep his tumor from growing would be useless. Tests had revealed that his initial diagnosis had now been elevated to stage four glioblastoma.

Six months, maybe.

Radiation and chemo treatments should be scheduled immediately, they had said, "possibly" giving him a little more time. Every question Harry had asked of the multitude of specialists that rotated through the door always answered with either "maybe" or "possibly."

Six months, possibly.

But the fact was the cancer, which had dug tentacle-like roots into normal brain tissue, was too deep and located too closely to critical brain regions for any kind of survival. He would die no matter what. The doctors also suggested seeking out specialized cancer centers, but they did so with little enthusiasm.

Six months, maybe.

In short, the doctors advised Harry to find something that brought him joy or pleasure and purpose, and focus his efforts entirely on that.

Easy to suggest, hard to do with the way things were going.

Six months, possibly.

CHAPTER ELEVEN

A good clean shooting

"WHO DO WE have here?" asked Lyndi, pulling on her latex gloves and squatting near the open driver's side door of an older model but custom built four-door Chevy Impala. A menacing reflection bounced from the flashing lights of the surrounding police vehicles off the Impala's twenty-two inch chrome rims momentarily causing her to squint and scowl.

The cops and first responders standing nearby who didn't know the detective, may have thought she was grimacing at the sight of the dead bodies in the car. But Lyndi Carnes had no problem with dead bodies, young or old, male or female, torn up or shot through, innocently killed or negligently. She was merely annoyed by the visual intrusion.

"Well, the big dude is a guy who goes by the nickname Jolly. We're still not sure on his real name. We're still awaiting a positive ID on the driver, but he's also known muscle. Back there laid out is none other than Killer Joe Elston," said a male officer in plainclothes, while uncomfortably adjusting his bulletproof vest, "reputed leader of the Black Disciples street gang."

"Yeah? So maybe a rival got to the snake's head," said Lyndi.

This shouldn't take too long.

"Well, you cut off a turkey's head and it still has some life left," answered the officer. "Who knows, this could be the start of something more than just a shootout."

Lyndi had stopped listening. This was impressive, she thought, staring into the vehicle. Usually a gang shooting resulted in bullet holes riddled everywhere, up and down quarter and door panels, across alleyways, embedded in trees, in mailboxes, in garbage cans, light posts far down the road. The perp frantic with a semi-automatic, in a hurry and scared, not aiming just firing, hoping to hit his target. This car wasn't rammed with an SUV or anything else to get it to stop, another common practice by gangbangers. The gear shift was in park, the engine off, the car body unblemished, no bullet holes in this slick, silver and tricked-out ride.

"Quite the wheels," Lyndi commented.

"Yeah," answered the officer, appearing bemused that she hadn't been listening to him. He looked at her peculiarly. Lyndi could sense he was perplexed on why she wasn't sweating, or glistening. He wiped his brow and glanced at her forehead, then at her chest.

"A good clean shooting," she said to herself, while peering into the backseat at the dark red splotch on Joe Elston's chest.

"Not a scratch on this two-tone metal flake paint job," said the officer, holding his belt with two hands. "A cousin of mine had his Dodge Charger painted this color awhile back and now I bet it's got more dimples than a golf ball."

Lyndi focused her attention on the bodies. Two with bullet wounds to the head, and Killer Joe with one directly in the chest. All at close range.

She glanced at the body in the backseat.

He shot you first, Joe, his main target. You look surprised. Your two buddies made some type of movement. You thought you could trust someone didn't you?

Joe Elston's head rested on plush white interior, a smatter of blood on both sides of his torso. His eyes and his mouth open. His tattooed arms lay at his sides, hands palms up.

The driver was bent over and leaning into the gap between his and the passenger's seats. Skull fragments were embedded in the lining of the roof's interior. His right hand jutted out from his body. Blood sat in the palm—no doubt, figured Lyndi, pooled there from the rivulet that streamed down his head, neck, shoulder and arm. He had possibly been reaching for something.

Probably the trunk lever.

Lyndi leaned further into the car and noticed a trunk release just a few inches from the driver's fingertips.

You trusted someone so much, Killer Joe, you didn't get your guns out of the trunk before you met with him.

The large man in the passenger seat was stooped against the window, the pinky and ring fingers of his right hand still wedged in the door handle.

You were headed to the trunk as well.

Lyndi reached in and pulled the trunk lever and watched it pop open.

The viaduct where the car sat was now teeming with officers. A small crowd was gathering behind crime scene tape at both ends of the bridge. Lyndi made her way behind the car before stopping. She stood there listening through the mumbles, the distant sirens, the screams of the summer cicadas. She looked up to see the officer staring at her. He quickly darted his eyes away. He's cute, she thought, but too young.

She could hear a rumbling sound emanating far down the tracks. She caught the eye of a district commander in uniform and hollered over to him.

"I need that train stopped before it gets here. Soot from this rusted out bridge might contaminate any prints we take off the vehicle."

She looked in the trunk and saw a cache of weapons, mostly handguns, all semi-automatics, some with extended clips. There were four or five in each of two fire-hose leather tool bags.

The officer joined her at the back of the car and peered into the trunk. "Wow, they were going to a party." He turned toward her, "I'm Sergeant Dave Flisk, from the Gang Enforcement Unit. I don't believe we've met." He reached out his hand to shake and Lyndi only squinted at him. His smile looked more flirtatious than friendly, his lips a little too pursed for the delayed introduction. She glanced at her latex evidence gloves and shrugged.

"Well, Dave Flisk, again, what do we have here?"

"These poor sons-of-bitches likely got taken out by the Two-Sixers on account of their boys selling this far south of Forty-Eighth Street. But it looks like they were heading out to a showdown before that happened." He scratched his head. "Not sure. This is Hispanic gang battleground we're in. What Killer Joe's doing here is anyone's guess."

He grinned, and Lyndi watched his eyes go to her chest again, and then to her hips, and then back to her face. She wasn't surprised. She could tell he was the kind of man who had sex on his brain all the time, not just every nine seconds or whatever it was. He was young, though the finely trimmed beard made him look older and more mature.

"You have a possible suspect, Flisk?"

Flisk shrugged his shoulders. "Likely one of The Scraper's boys. We've got a couple of CI's in there. I'll ask around. Can I get your cellphone number?"

Just then another officer, this one in a blue jumpsuit with Crime Scene Technician emblazoned in white across the back, approached and began photographing the scene. Lyndi's cellphone rang. She held up a finger to Flisk.

"Detective Lyndi Carlson."

"LC, it's Myles. What do you have there?"

"Someone that goes by the name Killer Joe Elston, leader of the Black Disciples and a couple of his associates, resting peacefully in a car. You?"

"We may have to double-down. I'm in a vestibule on Forty-Ninth and Winchester with Larry, Curly and Simon, Simon Gutierrez, also known as," Lyndi said the name at the same time, "The Scraper." Her partner continued, "Also known as the general of the," Lyndi again said the name aloud, "Two-Sixers."

"Well, that's a draw," she replied. "He's a potential suspect in this one. Tough night for gang leaders in Chicago. He doesn't happen to have a bullet hole in the chest, does he?"

"That and his throat cut to the bone. Two of his armed men look to have been shot in the head at point-blank range. No witnesses of course. Also, there's a small, thin smear of blood on the glass here, a few inches long, up and down, almost as if it were placed there by the perp. Probably cut himself. These guys are so stupid, LC. They might as well leave a photo I.D."

"I'll stick around and watch forensics do their thing and meet you at the coroner's office to compare and contrast vics."

Lyndi ignored officer Flisk's wide-eyed surprise at the name she mentioned on the phone and walked over to the side of the car, circling around the back bumper slowly, studying the maroon pinstripe along the front quarter panels and then across the hood. When she got to the front of the car there it was: A smear of blood, this one horizontal instead of vertical like the one Myles had described, no larger than the tip of someone's index finger and no longer than a few inches.

Lyndi told the CSI tech to take a photograph, and to be sure to get a swab of the blood for DNA analysis. He could have easily missed it, the smear somewhat blending in with the pinstripes.

One dead gang leader and a vertical streak of blood, and another with a horizontal streak. Now this is looking more like my kind of party.

She opened up a notebook and began jotting down notes.

CHAPTER TWELVE

Aint nobody innocent in Back of the Yards

WHEN HIS FAMILY finally stopped pestering him about moving, perhaps west, maybe further south, or up north, and stopped coming around altogether for fear for their lives, Jebediah Hatch bought a gun.

It was a nice looking gun and it was legal. He had filled out all the paperwork, went through all the background checks, attended the mandatory classes, waited the appropriate amount of time. Jebediah carried his Kimber 1911 Compact Stainless Steel II in a holster attached to his waistband in front of his back. The Firearm Concealed and Carry Act became state law in Illinois on July 9, 2013. It was perfectly alright for Jebediah to walk around with his handgun, though the copious No Gun signs in store windows always made him feel a little shameful. He proceeded into such stores believing that if he ever had to use the gun, his ignoring the sign would be least of the worries of the person who put the sign in the window in the first place.

Jebediah never went anywhere without his gun.

"It's done spread. There's no spreading, Pete. Gang-fightin and gunfire, the two go hand-in-hand 'round here nowadays. Has for a long time now. Damn shame. This neighborhood? You and I both remember when they closed the damn stockyards, out went the jobs, out went the Slovaks, in came the Mexicans and in come us. It was a nice place once. We lived in harmony. Now, look at it? Hell, makes me so angry I don't want to talk about it."

Jebediah turned away and looked down the street, toward the corner where just days before, in front of a ramshackle of a convenience store, a gang shooting resulted in what the media had referred to as "the death of an innocent bystander." Jebediah thought about that for a moment.

Aint nobody innocent in Back of the Yards.

Bloodstains, encircled by yellow crime scene tape whipping from a light summer breeze, remained on the sidewalk.

"Yeah, I know what you mean Jebediah. Bernie sold, Momma Jones over there done sold, the Jiminezs' sold—well, guess they didn't sell, but run off in the night. They use that flat for all sorts of goings on nowadays, aint they?" Pete squinted into the sun, looking hard past Jebediah's front porch and across the yards.

"Yeah, aint nothin good going on in that house, Pete. Hispanic gang, Latin Kings, have that locked down. Raymond Delgado running that show," answered Jebediah.

Pete, a heavyset man in trousers and a T-shirt damp with sweat, stood up, looking at Jebediah peculiarly.

"You know the names of the gangs and the guys in the gangs, Jebediah?"

Jebediah nodded, not turning toward his friend, just gazing out at the street, watching a large woman push a stroller, talk on her cellphone and eat food from a box.

Jebediah sighed. *I feel sorry for the babies of this world.*

He quickly snapped to another thought. "Pete, it aint the same as it was. Theys no respect anymore. Young men nowadays roam the streets, there pants hanging down past their asses. No jobs, no ambition. Think the world is at their beckon call. Think life is about money and the almighty bling, the fancy car, the gold chains. If they can't be a rapper or a basketball star, they gotta be in a gang. It's just the gang, the drugs, the guns, the women, the music and the money. They care about nothin else." He scowled. "It's gotten ugly."

After a lengthy pause, Pete broke the silence, "Well, it don't look like any mean streets today," he said, wiping the sweat from his brow. "There's lil kids playin down there in a sprinkler and someone down on the corner looks to be barbecuing."

"They like cockroaches, Pete. Come out in the dark, feast on what they can find," said Jebediah coldly. "Same thing going on in Pilsen, Little Village and over in Englewood. Last Halloween they shot a young mother walking with her kids, trick and treatin. Shot her dead. Gawdawful. Shameful."

Pete waved his hand. "Well, glad my son helped me get out while I could. Now, I said I'd check in on you, so now I'll be checking out, back to Portage Park where I don't have to fear gettin struck by a wayward bullet. You know what I mean?"

Pete chuckled and put on his Martin straw hat. He studied Jebediah. "You know, Portage Park is turnin into a nice place, Jebediah. You should come out some time. They got some nice bungalows out there. Every one of them someone lives in. No plywood over any windows. No trash in the streets. No vacant lots. Nobody doing something they shouldn't be doing. Just good people. You're still young enough to make a good life out there. The grandkids come visit you."

"I'll die here, Pete," replied Jebediah, gruffly, the grizzled look in his face appearing more pronounced.

"Oh c'mon, now. You too mean to die, Jebediah."

The men chuckled and shook hands, Jebediah's grip a vice to Pete's—thirty years of brick masonry work will do that. Jebediah may have been seventy years old but he was a solid muscular seventy-year-old. His wife, Adelae, died of heart disease four years earlier. That's the only time his children had ever seen him cry.

While lightly rocking in his front porch chair, Jebediah watched his friend Pete walk down the steps and get into his car. But he wasn't thinking about his friend.

"Raymond Delgado," Jebediah muttered, "your day will come."

CHAPTER THIRTEEN

Don't let them see that you're scared

IT WAS DUSK and the summer heat that had peaked near ninety-six degrees late in the afternoon had yet to let up. The guy they called Tin Can stood on the corner of West Forty-Eighth and Ashland, looking suspicious. He loitered about the corner, fidgeting with his brown trousers underneath a long cream-colored T-shirt. As a Volkswagen pulled up, he rubbed his chin and peered about, looking at the four corners. He leaned near the window of the car briefly and then pointed to a kid on a bike down the street.

"Suspect's gonna make a drop," said Flisk into the walkie-talkie receiver on the shoulder of his bullet proof vest. "Older model gray Volkswagen, likely gonna pay the skinny kid on the bike and probably circle. Be advised."

A gruff, authoritative voice came back, "Flisk, you and Boggs quietly take Tin Can and the Volks. We've got the kid on the bike."

"Roger that."

Flisk wiped the sweat from his forehead. The Volkswagen slowed, a white arm reached out and handed a wad of cash to the kid, who quickly took it and shoved it into his pocket and began to ride his bike east on Forty-Eighth, following the Volkswagen before it turned in front of him.

When the Volkswagen came back around the block, Flisk had put the unmarked car in drive and was slowly approaching the intersection. Tin Can wasn't too smart, wasn't too arrogant, wasn't too brave. He'd been in this predicament before. Flisk had arrested him for possession with intent to sell a year or so before. But the gangs were engulfed in a bloody turf war now and who knows for sure what Tin Can was carrying. One thing Flisk knew, Tin Can had kept fidgeting with his trousers.

Boggs hit the lights—red and blue flashes popping from the dash, the grille and the back window of the car. Flisk positioned the vehicle in front of the Volkswagen. He trained his eye on Tin Can, studying his reaction to their sudden presence. Only briefly did he look at the young men in the Volkswagen. All he needed to see was their surprise and he knew they weren't going anywhere.

Tin Can spooked, "Shit!" and started to run.

As he bounded out of the car, Flisk spoke into his walkie-talkie. "We've got a ten-forty-one. In foot pursuit of suspect west on Forty-Eighth."

Young and in shape, Flisk was fast on his feet, but the heat forced him to use all he had in the initial pursuit. He was soon out of breath and could feel his legs turning heavy.

Tin Can was having no problems with the heat. His only trouble was his trousers, he kept his hand pressed against something at his gut when he ran, while the back of his pants fell down, revealing dirty white briefs.

Not too bright, Tin Can, thought Flisk as his suspect made a turn on Marshfield instead of Paulina. Flisk pinched his walkie-talkie again and tried to get out the words in-between breaths.

"Suspect heading south on Marshfield. Wait, fuck! Down a gangway, west now in the alley."

Despite the restrictiveness due to his pants, Tin Can was quite lithe and agile. He hurdled a small chain-link fence and zigged-zagged around some cars on the street, then burst through a backyard, a garage, the alley, another garage, and another backyard before zipping south on Paulina, in the opposite direction of officer Boggs.

Flisk stayed on his tail forty or so yards behind, but as he looked up while coming around a car, he noticed that Tin Can was no longer wearing the long cream colored shirt and no longer holding up his pants. He also looked to be carrying a silver-plated gun. Immediately, Flisk drew his service weapon with his right hand and pinched the walkie-talkie with his left while trying desperately to pick up his speed. "Suspect armed heading south on …" The sweat. The blurred vision. The heat was getting to him. He tried to blink it away. "South on …"

He caught a glimpse of Tin Can darting from the open street down a gangway.

"West in the middle of Paulina or … toward alley." Flisk's words were drowned out immediately as a deep bass beat came quickly into hearing range followed by staccato lyrics to a rap song.

He did his best to ramp up his pursuit as he approached the gangway. He was hoping to catch Tin Can before he entered another backyard. The sweat had grown thick on him now and his legs were wilting. He wasn't sure exactly how far they had gone.

Huffing and puffing, he kicked open a wood gate and raised his weapon at the shirtless man standing before him.

"Freeze, police! Hands up! Hands up! Show me your hands!" He swung the gun to another man and yet another man, and then a group of men and women, all glaring at him, the beat of the bass pulsating with the ache in his head.

"Hands! Hands! Everybody's hands up!" The sweat spit from his mouth as Flisk drew a breath of barbecue smoke."

"Fuck you, man. You can't come in here disruptin my party!"

The crowd mumbled its agreement and everyone seemed to move in a hostile manner.

Flisk knew it was that same feeling again but this time layered with something more tangible. He hadn't been able to describe it to the therapist. She had said it was simple fear, a distressing emotion. To Flisk it was more than that, perhaps something like fear and self-doubt melded together to form some new incapacitating emotion. He felt instantly vulnerable.

The rap song ended as the meat on the barbecue sizzled.

They don't know you. They don't know you.

"Hey!"

Flisk aimed his gun up on a porch where a shirtless man in jeans and unlaced boots stood glaring down at him. The man was flanked by two scantily clad women. He seemed to have an arm around both.

"This is a *fiesta*, bitch! Now you take yer punk ass outta here and let us—"

"I'm in pursuit …"

That's it Dale—Dave. You're in pursuit of a suspect. You need everyone to cooperate for a moment while you take a look around. Tell them to keep their hands where you can see them. Don't let them see that you're scared. Now, say it!

"I'm in pursuit of a suspect, who came in—" His walkie-talkie crackled, "Flisk, where you at?"

Flisk caught the tattoo in his line of sight now, stamped on the left pectoral of the man standing on the porch, a five-point crown.

Shit, they'd ran a few blocks more than he had thought. He stuttered. "What's the … the … where are we? What's the …" He pinched his walkie-talkie, "Paulina … er Marshfield … West of Paulina. Requesting backup—uh, Code Twenty, Code Twenty. I repeat Code Twenty."

His arm was getting tired and the crowd had begun to move in defiance.

A step back would bring more defiance. A step forward would fuel the anger.

Flisk braced himself and held the gun out rigidly.

"Suspect was shirtless, spotted sellin on the corner, likely a Gangster Disciple," he said, figuring what the hell, maybe it'd put them all at ease knowing he wasn't in pursuit of one of their own.

"Aint no disciple live too long in this backyard."

Flisk wasn't sure who had said it. The men began milling about, smirking at one another. The man on the porch stepped down and walked through the crowd closer to Flisk. His fists were clinched and his head was slightly bowed.

Flisk finally recognized him, Raymond Delgado, head of the Latin Kings. He looked pissed.

Shit.

Flisk didn't point the gun directly at him, just held it out, pretending to scan the crowd but keeping Delgado in his peripheral.

"A white cop lookin to kill another black dude!" Someone in the crowd yelled.

"You aint lookin for no disciple," said Delgado. "You're just hear to harass me some more. What is it with you, man? Do I do it for you? Is that it?"

"He was sellin. We're in pursuit … He took off on us. I just need your cooperation."

Seconds later, officer Boggs came into view from the opposite end of the yard, his weapon holstered, his large hands shoving men out of his way. He walked nonchalantly.

"What the fuck you doing, Flisk? C'mon man, I crushed Tin Can in the alley. Got him in the backseat. His piece is in the trunk."

"Tell that homie he come round here again it won't be the cops that get him," said Delgado. He turned and pointed at Flisk. "And I better not see you around here again, neither."

Boggs turned toward Delgado. "Is that a threat? Because we can take you in on a threat and you'll miss yer lil party you're havin here."

"That just what you want, yo, shoot you a Latino dead at a party."

A wail of sirens descended on the block and a helicopter swooshed in, circling above, its blades chopping through the bass of the music that had erupted again.

Boggs glanced upward in surprise and then turned to Flisk with a look of reproach. "What the fuck did you do, man, call in the cavalry?"

CHAPTER FOURTEEN

That brings to 36 ...

News Report

Weekend full of gun violence
21 shot during 11-hour stretch

CHICAGO WAS HIT with a burst of gun violence over the scorching weekend with at least 21 people shot during an 11-hour stretch from Friday evening into Saturday morning, according to police.

That brings to 36 the number of people who have been shot in the city since Wednesday afternoon, when two women were hit by gunfire as they sat on a porch just a block from Garfield Park on the West Side.

The shootings have stretched across the city but have been concentrated in the South and West sides. The Englewood and Harrison districts have both seen a handful of people shot over the last two days, and there have been shootings as far south as the Altgeld Gardens neighborhood at the edge of the city to the Rogers Park neighborhood bordering Evanston.

Three of those wounded were shot by police officers in Back of the Yards, Rogers Park and Englewood. The man shot in Englewood, around 9:50 p.m., died.

In one of the shootings Friday night, gunfire was exchanged between cars, injuring at least one person in each car, police said.

The shooting occurred around 10:50 p.m. near the 1100 block of South Pacific Avenue, police said. A 23-year-old woman was shot in the arm and back and was stable at Chicago Medical Center. A 22-year-old man was shot in the leg and neck and was in serious condition at the same hospital.

CHAPTER FIFTEEN

How do you want to die?

I WENT THROUGH all the stages. Denial. Anger. Bargaining. Depression. Acceptance.

I didn't get to acceptance easily. After ignoring the headaches, the blurred vision, the unsteadiness, the fatigue, going on with life despite that anvil on my shoulder or in my head, I got pissed off and punched a lot of walls, kicked over a lot of chairs, spit out a lot of curse words. I drank a fifth of Jack Daniels and I rarely drink hard liquor. And then I fell into a heap of blubbering tears on the couch.

I begged God, Moses, Jesus, Mary, Paul, or whoever was currently managing this mortal coil to spare my life. I said I'd be the best person that ever lived if you just let me continue to live. The sun appeared on what had been a rainy day and I thought just maybe somebody was listening. A possible sign. But then the clouds rolled back over, shadows canvassed the streets, and it was pouring again by evening time. So I said fuck it and went to a bar on 18th Street and got drunk again—this time on beer.

The next day, hungover but terminally ill to care, I entered into the acceptance stage. I did a lot of reading. One blog post from a mother who cared for her four-year-old daughter who had a similar terminal brain cancer, stuck with me. The kid had no clue what dying meant, and that was both a sad thing and a good thing. Reading that mother's first-person account of her child suffering through the treatments and then the effects of the cancer itself, how it slowly rendered the poor kid into a vegetative state before killing her, broke my heart.

I was soon cursing myself for my selfishness. I had been given forty-two years in this world. That kid got four years. I had no reason to feel sorry for myself. I remember thinking that I was glad the kid was never able to experience the kind of evil that exists in this world. Still, I cried my eyes out.

And then I watched a video of a young woman who had decided to end her life before the terminal cancer did it for her, sparing her from excruciating pain and sparing her loved ones the memory of her imminent decline. She was diverging from the course. It was courageous. Shutting off the lights on her own terms. Took guts. Why should she allow a cancerous tumor in her brain to decide her fate? It was her life. She was a twenty-nine year-old California girl, newly married. She died in Oregon because of the state's Death with Dignity Act. I cried my eyes out on that one, too.

So, I asked myself, "Harry, how do you want to die?" What course of action will you take? Will you go out with dignity and grace?

Well, how will that be possible when you're suffering debilitating seizures, shitting your pants and not remembering anyone or anything?

No, I didn't think I wanted to do that.

Will you go out by "accidently" slipping and falling off a cliff in Honolulu after maxing out your credit cards on the finest extravagances? Or, pick up and abruptly leave your friends and Lyndi, and move to another state that allows this "Death with Dignity" and suck down a few pills and drift away?

No, I didn't want to do that, either.

But what about both? I could do both, exactly what that four-year-old girl did and exactly what that twenty-nine year-old woman did.

I'd fight on my own terms and try to die that way too, with a sense of peace in my heart. If I could just get there.

-HJW

CHAPTER SIXTEEN

He stepped into the sunlight of the day

HARRY WEST TOLD his bosses that he blamed his health issues on the pressure of his job. He said that on the inside he had grown increasingly cynical and sullen over the years, while on the outside he maintained a façade of contentment. He also told them he had finally grown tired of defending hardened criminals and witnessing the ineptitude and the power abuse of public servants in the judicial system. He was referring to them and they knew it.

In explaining his recent episode in the courtroom, he used the words "depleted," "overextended" and "fatigued," before closing with the statement, "Plain and simple, I'm burnt out."

He mentioned that his doctor's analysis indicated a possible correlation with burnout and two other mental health conditions: anxiety and depression.

Harry West told his bosses about his personal life but not everything. He explained his relationship with Chicago Homicide Detective Lyndi Carlson, admitting that it was probably a conflict of interest in regards to his job. He revealed to them that he had been experiencing anxiety spells when considering the possibility of asking Lyndi to be his wife. The anxiety, he figured, derived from his doubt that she would actually accept his proposal. It was partly true. He had wanted to marry her, but that was before he finally accepted his fate.

In Harry's eyes it just didn't seem Lyndi's nature to ever be married. Not when she wouldn't even consider herself a girlfriend. Some of the stress that compounded with his job came from that uncertainty. He did not want to lose Lyndi Carnes. His bosses had nodded agreeably. They had seen or heard about the beautiful homicide detective. When they glanced at one another, their eyebrows had gone up in unison and their faces had simultaneously, though only momentarily, flushed red.

Harry neglected to tell his bosses about the terminal brain cancer diagnosis.

He carried the box full of personal mementos he had gathered from his office down a long corridor of cubicles, past eyes of sympathy, indifference and pity. He stepped out into the sunlight of the day, and walked to the parking garage.

Harry had a lot to do in the waning days of his life.

CHAPTER SEVENTEEN

Like a dog

"YOU'RE HERE TO cook me my food, keep the trailer tidy. You do that and I'll give you a bone when I want to give you a bone. Do you understand that, Fat Annie?"

When she nodded, Leroy Crump loosened his grip on the dog collar around Annie's neck. She slowly began to rise up from the floor but he kicked her back down. "Nah, you stay on all fours rest of the day. Everything you do you gonna do on all fours, like a dog. You hungry, dog? Ah, what am I askin for, you're always hungry. Hereya are …"

He scooped up a handful of mashed potatoes and slapped them down on the floor. "Eat!" When she hesitated he scooped up another handful of potatoes and threw it down at her head. With her hands, she began eating the food off the trailer floor.

"With your mouth, like a dog!" He hollered.

He settled back into his chair and began to pick at a meal. "When my brothers want to eat, you ask me first if it's okay for you to make'em somethin. If they want to fuck, you tell me they want it, and I'll gut them hole to hole, because nobody fucks my Fat Annie dog unless I says so. You got that?"

He watched her head nod as she continued to eat the food off the floor. "Here, you want somethin to drink with that, doggy?" Crump picked up a can of beer and poured some of it on her head. "Now, look up and get yourself somethin to wash it down with."

When she turned her head upward he poured the can again—the beer splashing over her face and mouth. "Go on get some, doggy" he said, laughing sinisterly. "Go on."

Annie stuck out her tongue and sloshed at the beer pouring down her face.

"That's it," said Crump. "Thata girl."

CHAPTER EIGHTEEN

Adjusting

DAVE FLISK STUMBLED drunkenly into the kitchen, his eyes grasping at blurry images, his hands trembling, his legs teetering. He was sweating profusely.

"Are you drunk, D?" April, his wife, called him D. She had to. Couldn't bring herself to call him by his new name. Wouldn't even consider calling him by his old name.

"No, baby. I've just had a bad day."

"It's four in the mornin," she said standing at the entrance to the kitchen in a long, wrinkly T-shirt draped over her thin shoulders and hanging down to her thighs.

"I know what time it is. I had a rough shift and I went out with the guys afterwards, and I'm … could you jes … jes let me be?"

The faint sound of a baby crying caused them both to glare at each other until they were red in the face.

She spoke first. "Does it make it any better to go get drunk? Does it?"

"You know nothin, April, so leave it at that and let me make a grilled-cheese-sandwich!" he spit back, opening and slamming cabinets, looking for a skillet.

"What do you mean, D? I was there. I know it all. I went through it too, you know. Now Daniella is going through it." She pointed behind her as if the baby was sitting right there. "You rarely sleep. You rarely talk to me." She took a deep breath and began to cry. "I gave birth four months ago and you haven't touched me since … since before that, D!"

"April, honey, all I want to do is make a god-damned-grilled-cheese," pans fell out of a cabinet, clanking on the tiled floor as he continued to rummage for the skillet, "fuckin-sandwich! Now leave me alone!"

"I want a divorce."

Dave Flisk found the skillet but hurled it into the dining room where it disappeared into darkness before smashing against a wall, table and then the floor. "You want to divorce me! You want to divorce me! You want to fuckin divorce ME! After all the shit I've been through, now you want to take my family away from me?"

She put up her hands. "I can't take this anymore, D. You said things were going to be different up here. When you do come home, you're like a ghost in this house. It's like there's no soul left in you. We don't talk. We don't go out. I don't ever get to go out and have some drinks."

"Is that what you wanna do, April, put on one of your slutty little skirts again, pretend you aren't a mother and go out and get drunk?"

"Where is all this coming from, D?" She wiped her eyes and pointed at him. "You know, I'm beginning to think that two people died that day."

"Don't you even think about him." He pointed fiercely back at her. "So help me if you say his name. So help me!"

April's voice, moist and crackly, was barely audible. "D, I don't want to live like this."

The panic came back to Dave Flisk in a desperate wave. He wanted to wrap his arms around his young, sweet wife and squeeze her tightly. And he wanted to wrap his hands around her dainty, little neck and choke the life out of her.

She had suffered through a lot. It was the front lawn of her parents' home that a horde of reporters camped out on, waiting for a glimpse of or for a statement from "the fiancée" of the cop in question. She had stood by him. But now this? Wanting a divorce? Telling him at four in the morning. He knew he wasn't easy to live with. It was going to take time. That's what the therapists had repeated over and over again. "Adjusting," will take time.

Adjusting. They called it, adjusting.

The new commander was an asshole. The gangs were at war. The gangs were always at war. He couldn't trust his instincts anymore. He couldn't trust himself. There was a storm in his head, a flood in his heart. How could he protect his family if they leave him? How could he protect himself if he had no reason to?

He approached her in a threatening manner, hissing and blowing air heavily through his nostrils.

She stood her ground as the baby's cries strengthened. "I'm not afraid of you, D," she said quietly, pushing in her lips. "You don't scare me."

It's not what he wanted to see or hear. He wanted, at the very least, to see a trace of fear in her eyes. He wanted her to flinch.

He looked at her chest, her drooping breasts outlining the thin T-shirt, and then at her legs. When he looked back up at her eyes, he noticed they had softened. She had blinked away the tears.

He reached over and grabbed the T-shirt at her waist and pulled her into him. She turned up her face and pulled back. "D," she said before allowing him to kiss her, first just pecks and then going at it strong.

The shirt went up above her waist and her panties went down to her ankles. He lifted her up by her thighs and she wrapped her legs around him.

"This changes nothing, D," she whispered.

"Shut-up, April," he said.

He carried her to the couch in the living room. She quickly went for his belt, unbuckled it, and shimmied his jeans down to his thighs with her hands and then with her feet.

Between the moans, the baby continued to cry.

CHAPTER NINETEEN

Struggling with some demons

News Report

Body of high school athlete found

Missing for days, 18-year-old's body found in abandoned house

THE BODY OF a Naperville North High School student-athlete was found in an abandoned house on the 400 block of Bishop Street in West Englewood.

Michael Aaron Coughlin, Jr, 18, of the 800 block of Florence Drive in Naperville, died of what is suspected to be a drug overdose, according to police.

Coughlin, a senior at Naperville North and an All-state pitcher, was last seen in his car near the corner of Seeley Avenue and 66th Street in Chicago on June 12. The vehicle, a 2015 Ford Mustang GT, has yet to be recovered.

"Right now this is a death investigation," said Chicago Police spokesperson Angela Dooley. "There's no preliminary evidence to suggest that Mr. Coughlin was the victim of a kidnapping or a homicide."

The discovery comes on the heels of Michael Coughlin, Sr., owner of the prestigious trading firm Coughlin and Associates, holding a press conference to scold the Chicago Police Department for not doing enough to locate his missing son, who the elder Coughlin had suggested was likely kidnapped for money.

Toxicology results are pending, but Dooley said physical evidence at the scene and in Coughlin's possession suggest the death occurred as a result of a heroin and cocaine overdose.

"So far, in our discussions with the coroner, there's been no indication of foul play in Mr. Coughlin's death," she said.

The 6-foot-4, 190-pound Coughlin was expected to attend Notre Dame in the fall and tryout for the baseball team, according to Bob Macado, his high school baseball coach.

"Michael was a great kid, a straight-A student and a heck of an athlete," added Macado. "He might have been struggling with some demons that no one new about. But he was the kind of kid that lit up every room he walked into."

Naperville North High School officials earlier this week issued a statement and extended condolences to Coughlin's family.

"We are saddened to learn of the passing of student Michael Coughlin, Jr.," Naperville North High School Principal Stephen McDanniel said in a statement. "The Naperville North community offers our sincere condolences to his family and friends during this difficult time." Plans are pending for a private wake and funeral to be

held for Coughlin, according to a Coughlin family statement.

CHAPTER TWENTY

It'll be my death

WHY I CHOSE not to tell anyone:

Well, there are many reasons but I'll make mention of three in particular.

One, I do not like to be pitied. And pitied I would have been for sure. Friends and family would have called, moaned, wept, patted me on the back, dropped off chicken casseroles, sent sympathy cards, wanted to take me here and there, give me advice on who to see, what to do next. Specialists in Minnesota. A spiritual healing clinic in Budapest. They'd try their best to comfort me. They'd tell me bad jokes, thinking they were lifting my spirits, and they'd reminisce something awful about the glory days.

In other words, they would have made life miserable for me.

I'd rather be dead than pitied. Besides, knowing would make them say and do things they normally wouldn't say and do. This way, they don't have to put on a sympathetic persona in my presence. It's phony anyway. You feel bad for the guy, sure, but then you're talking behind his back and blaming his situation on lifestyle or some other crap because you can't get your head around the fact that IT CAN JUST HAPPEN. All the while, you're thanking God it's not you in his shoes as you chomp on expensive red meat, drink fine wine and fuck what you can.

No pity parties. No sorrowful sendoffs. Just one day, wake up and who? Harry West? No longer here. Gone. A memory.

The second reason: Why send friends and family down such a dark road, a road that ends with my end? Could have been the day I told them, the next day or four to six months down the road. They'd suffer right along with me. Why put them through that pain? Why make them feel as if they were the one dying? Would you wish such suffering on a loved one, a friend, a spouse, on anyone? It'd even be a tough thing to wish upon your worst enemies.

Thirdly, I didn't want to be a burden on anyone. I didn't want anyone having to change my diaper or wipe my ass or clip my nose hair or pretend to talk to me about a beautiful day when I'm sitting in a hospital gown shitting myself, foaming at the mouth and mumbling incoherently. I didn't want anyone bathing me, brushing my teeth, watching my body become paralyzed and no longer work as it was intended.

If I had let Lyndi in on the little secret, a part of me thinks she would have said goodbye to good ole Harry

West. Not for fear of the unknown, but for lack of interest. What future could I provide her? Zip. I had no future. My future was here and now, maybe tomorrow, maybe not. Is a dying man interesting to a woman who has such a zest for life?

I couldn't afford to lose her. I needed to soak in that amazing woman as much as possible before the light went dim. If she knew, she might have changed. Emotionally, physically, spiritually. I couldn't take that chance. She's perfect the way she is, living free of despair. I wanted to go out seeing that, feeling that.

Dying also meant that it was time to start doing things you never would have had an inclination of doing when you were living.

It's my life. It'll be my death.

-HJW

CHAPTER TWENTY-ONE

Evil be everywhere

THE CAR GARBLED past again, slowing to a near stop, its engine clunking and sputtering. This was the fourth time in twenty or so minutes, thought Jebediah, peering out an upper floor window of his home. When the car rolled into the yellow hue of the street light, it looked to be gray in color. It was old, a Camaro, gray and rusty.

An unusual car even for this neighborhood. Think I'll take a closer look.

Jebediah made his way down the stairs, unlatched the deadbolt on his front door and stepped out onto the porch. The night air was still but warm. He made his way down the porch steps and approached the car.

"Hey," Jebediah tapped on the window, "roll down yer window, boy." He tapped again, and then again.

Finally, the driver's side door opened and a large man stood up, looking at Jebediah as if he were nothing but a mere nuisance.

"What you keep driving by for?" Asked Jebediah, trying to make out the splotches on the man's neck, face and head in the dark. The streetlight was too dim.

"What's your name, grandpa?"

"My name's none of yer business. Now, I asked you a question. You don't look as if you got any business here, so maybe I should call the police."

"You know who lives over in that there house?" he pointed to a two-flat down the road.

Jebediah looked at the two-flat and processed it was the old Jiminez's place, now occupied by Raymond Delgado and his street gang, the Latin Kings. Jebediah seethed.

"You lookin to buy drugs? You go, get on out of this neighborhood." He hobbled to the front of the Camaro. "I mean it, you needs to go before …" Jebediah stopped abruptly. "Is that a blasted swastika on yer neck? Jesus H. Christ, man! Who you think you are, comin in this here neighborhood with ink like that on yerself?"

The man softly shut the door of the car and looked around. The street was quiet. Jebediah took a step back.

"I aint leavin just yet, grandpa" said the man.

"Look, I don't want no trouble. I just askin you to be on your way is all."

"The trouble began when you were born. It escalated when you tapped on my window."

Jebediah braced his legs. He felt the weight of his Kimber 1911 handgun behind him at his waist. He assured himself he'd use it if need be. "I may look old and yer big enough, but I'll still whup you, boy," he said, staring at the man, chin out.

"I think I need to remind you your place, grandpa." The man reached down, unlatched his belt and yanked it through the straps of his jeans. Rolling it up until the big silver buckle was firm around his right knuckles, he moved quickly toward Jebediah.

There was nowhere to go, and nothing he could do but throw up one bony arm for protection before the blow smashed in his glasses and knocked him back onto the pavement. A kick to his side flipped him over onto his stomach before the lashes violently cracked across his back in quick succession. Jebediah let out a horrific croak at each one, his wire-framed glasses crumpled and teetering on the bridge of his nose, blood oozing from a nostril. He looked up in a daze and saw people standing around, watching. The man whipping and beating him must have noticed them too, because he stopped momentarily, his laughter waning into the night.

"You bout to kill that *viejo*," said a man standing in the street, ensconced in the darkness outside the streetlight's coverage.

The man with the belt started to laugh again. This time more sinisterly. "That's right!" He said. "I hate these worthless sacks of shit!" The man came down hard with the belt against Jebediah's back.

"But, yo, you aint gonna kill that old man here in my hood. Who you roll with?"

"Who the fuck are you?"

"You watch how you talk to Raymond Delgado," said another voice from the darkness. "Who you rollin with?"

The man began to back away toward his Camaro, looking around to how many men were in his vision line. Jebediah turned his head and swiped off his broken glasses. He could see the man didn't look scared, more surprised if anything. The asshole was considering something. That's when Jebediah pushed himself up and jerked the Kimber out of its holster from his back and pointed it at the man near the Camaro. "Yer gonna go straight to the pokey or straight to hell for whippin me like a dog in the street!"

"By the looks of it, I'm already in hell," said the man, followed by another sinister laugh.

Someone from the darkness told Jebediah to put away the gun. "Or I'll let him kill you here in the street."

After a few seconds the man at the Camaro became impatient and gaited toward Jebediah, whose hands began to tremble. Jebediah took three steps back and recoiled downward. The man snatched the gun from his hands and tossed it toward the voice in the darkness, the metal hitting the cement with a clank. He then turned around and walked back to the Camaro, got in and fired up the sputtery engine. As his car trundled past the men in the street, he yelled from the window, "I'm with the Nation, baby!" and left them with the sinister laugh trailing behind.

Jebediah sat in the street breathless, whimpering until a man stood over him. He looked up and saw Raymond Delgado holding his gun and looking down at him.

"I coulda let that big boy waste you, *viejo*," he said. "Now maybe you stop being such a grumpy old man all the time, and understand that havin the Kings round is a benefit." He tossed the gun into Jebediah's lap and started to walk back toward the two-flat.

"Yer … yer probably the reason he was here in the first place. If it wasn't for you sellin yer drugs this wouldn't have happened!" Jebediah had a notion to raise the gun and fire it at the back of Delgado's head, but like he did when confronted with the possibility of shooting the man with the swastika tattoos, he froze up and instead wept more intensely.

"What is this world comin to?" he muttered through his sobs. "Evil be everywhere." Shaking his head now, "Evil be … everywhere."

CHAPTER TWENTY-TWO

Skugs and Bolt do crank for breakfast

THE CRICKETS BLEATED in the silence of the night. Somewhere a trickle of water fell from the overpass onto the dead street below. The rails rattled in the distance, somewhere far off.

"How long were you in lockup, Tin Can?"

"Bout fourteen days."

"When's your next hearing?"

"I don't know, my aunt Lulah know, and she pissed."

"Well, I'll do what I can to get them to ease up on the charges, but I need something from you."

"Whoa, coppa, I don't suck no dick!"

"Good to know, but I need some info."

"What you need, man? Yis already done near killed my heart, chasing me like that into Latin King country. Sheeet."

"You know about the death of the rich suburban kid, right? The towheaded high school ballplayer all over the news?"

"Man, I don't watch the news."

"Bullshit. You know what I'm talking about. He bought some Black Pearl up around forty-seventh, but I can't pin-point from who with all the warring and shifting these days. I want to know what gang, specifically."

"Man, what you want to know that for? The last time I gave you some info like that, two homies ended up messed up."

"Fuck off, you ingrate! I don't answer any of your questions—you answer mine or I'm hauling your ass back in again. I could have *fed* you to those Latin Kings! You'd be eatin from a straw in the infirmary at Metro Correctional right now!"

"Alright, cheel, man. Skugs and Bolt was talkin bout that kid awhile back. Said he come by Skugs' crib, lookin to buy. Kid ended up buyin a dime's worth, man. Fifteen decks, somethin like that. Outrageous."

"He bought off those imbeciles? Skugs and Bolt do crank for breakfast."

"Nah, man, but Skugs he know all the dealers and they said the kid went off by hisself bought it off Pablo. And Pablo sell for Night Train and them Imperial Gangstas. Now, Johnny Night Train Ayalla, one bad muthafucker. I wouldn't go—"

"Yeah-yeah, they all think they're bad muthafuckers. I can take it from here, Tin Can. Now get out of the car."

"You got a CI in Night Train's crew, too?"

"We got CIs in every crew, dumbshit."

"Man, you gonna get them to knock it down to just a possession, aint you? I got priors, you know."

"Get out."

Tin Can flung the car door open in a rage. The rattling sound began to build. "Fuck you, Flisk! Fuck you and fuck your family!" His shouting was washed out by the overhead train, and the car's engine firing up and rumbling off.

CHAPTER TWENTY-THREE

What happens next?

THE RATTLE OF the elevated train, the warble of pigeons, the honk of taxis, the thunder of buses and cars trundling over the bridges.

He didn't hear any of it.

I don't want to care about it anymore.

It was in Harry's thoughts during some kayaking with Lyndi down the Chicago River. It had stayed with him for most of the day, repeating in his head, *I don't want to care about it anymore.*

The sun was shining, a cool breeze in the air. They had paddled through downtown, under the steel bridges and the elevated trains. Harry had watched the people hurrying to their destinations, headphones on, faces buried in cellphones, missing out on the beauty of the day. He had wondered if they knew where they were going. Really knew. Not just to work, or a friend's house, or home, or to a restaurant, but did they really know where they were ultimately headed? To the other side of the bridge. What was on the other side of the bridge? Was there anything on the other side of the bridge?

It was obvious that Lyndi had caught him staring at her a few times. He couldn't help himself, just trying to take in all the beauty he could.

"What are you thinking, Harry West?" she had hollered over to him from the north side of the river near the LaSalle Street bridge.

"What happens next," he had replied quietly to himself.

"What?" she probably thought he had said something funny. She was smiling, her teeth bright white as she went through the shadow of the bridge. She wore a maroon tank-top, her skin sunned a cool brown, her shades shimmering from the reflections off the water and the glass skyscrapers. She had showed up looking gorgeous as usual, her cinnamon-colored hair pulled back, in the tight tank, the tight Levi's, the pink sneakers. She rarely carried a purse, so Harry figured she wore long pants in the summer to conceal her gun. She always carried the damn thing.

She had turned her head his way, waiting eagerly for his witty comment. He liked that, meant she knew a lot about him and wasn't bored. Maybe she felt something for him. He wanted to tell her he loved her. Paddle over, grab her kayak, pull her in close, tell her and kiss her. But she'd no doubt be annoyed by the emotional outpouring and probably worry more that he was losing his mind.

"I said I have yet to see any floaters," he said.

She had continued to smile. "Give it time." Then, she had picked up her paddling and yelled, "Race you to the locks!" She took off, stabbing at the water and pulling her kayak forward.

He didn't pursue her, just watched her go. He didn't have the energy anyway. His arms were dead and he didn't feel like he was breathing effortlessly. He looked up on the bridge and noticed a young boy looking down at him. The boy was African American, and stood staring at Harry with no expression. A woman who looked to be his mother and a little girl, possibly his sister, were a few feet away looking up at the skyscrapers.

Harry put up his hand to say hello, but the boy just stood there looking down at him.

Will he grow up, get a good job, marry, raise a family, live a good life and die at an old age? Will he get caught up in a gang and wind up in jail or dead? Will he stay clear of gangs but get cut down by a stray bullet? Will he live awhile and then end up with some deadly disease and die relatively young?

I don't want to care about it anymore.

The kid continued to stare at him, the two of them locked in on each other.

The sounds of the city carried on: The rattle of the elevated train, the warble of pigeons, taxis honking, the thunder of buses and cars trundling over the bridges. And Lyndi calling to him, faintly from up the river.

"Where's the fight, Harry?"

He had put his hand back up to say goodbye to the young boy, and felt a wash of relief when the kid nodded.

*****

Lyndi wanted to drink a few beers. Harry wanted to go back to her place and cuddle up naked in bed. Lyndi said there's all night for that Harry West.

Well, Harry was fine with drinking a few beers then.

They watched the end of a Cubs game at Fado, an Irish pub on Grand Avenue. Lyndi had made mention of how quiet Harry was, but when he answered vaguely she didn't delve too deep into why. She figured it was the stress he was feeling in regards to his job—his former job—and what the future held. She sidled over to him in the booth and they clanked their pint glasses together.

"Slàinte," they both said and took gulps from their Guinness.

"To good health *and* to your future," added Lyndi, hoping maybe to goad Harry into talking about his plans, if there were any yet. But Harry only turned his head back up to the television in the corner.

"Hey, Harry," she said, "why don't you come down to the gym tomorrow, play some hoops with us. We could use another player."

"Yeah, maybe," Harry replied with a waning grin.

She watched him as he looked up at the television, something she'd never really done before, concentrating on his demeanor, his disposition, trying to parse what was going through his mind. She usually never wasted her time with such things.

Perhaps I'm evolving. Perhaps I could someday settle down. Perhaps not.

The waitress stopped by the table and she ordered a shot of Jameson Whiskey. She glanced at Harry to see if he wanted the same, but he declined. "Make it a double," Lyndi said anyway.

On the way home, she was craving a gyro and they stopped off at a corner hot dog joint near Clark Street. It was getting late and Harry seemed fidgety and appeared tired. They were outside waiting in a short line near picknick tables when a man in line began yelling at a woman

and her daughter across the street. The man seemed bel-
ligerent. He stepped out of line and tossed a water bottle
at the woman.

"What you doin out, bitch? Where you been, yuh?"
The man was big, wore a crooked ballcap, oversized
jeans and a white T-shirt. He lumbered across the street
toward the woman and her daughter, yelling and throwing his arms up. The woman was giving it right back to
him, cursing him out.

"You done been over to LaQuinta's crib, dope
Chawlie told me. So you can forget bout touchin me tonight." The woman, heavyset, pointed at her breasts and
wagged a finger at the man. Her daughter lagged behind,
carrying a doll.

"Fuck you, you fat bitch," said the man now up in
the woman's face, pushing her with his body against the
brick wall of an abandoned warehouse. He began to
shove the woman as they went around a corner, out of
sight.

Lyndi sighed and turned to Harry but he wasn't
there. He was walking toward the corner. "What are you
doing, Harry?" she called out to him.

"Hey!" Harry hollored, while crossing the street and
turning the corner.

The big man either didn't hear him or ignored him
altogether. "You know where I been fat ugly hoe bitch?
I been at yer sister's fistin and slappin that. That's right!"
They had made it about a half block away.

"Hey!" Harry was behind the couple now. "Knock
it off for the sake of the child."

The big man briefly turned his head, "Mind yer own
business, faggot!"

Harry grabbed the man's shoulder and spun him
around, then felt his stomach cave in and the air in his

lungs leave his body. He dropped to his knees, gasping. Lyndi was soon next to him, crouching in the street, trying to help him up.

"Yo Foxy, when you done with limp dick here, you should come hang with a real man."

"He aint no real man," said the woman. "I have a better time with myself than with him."

Harry managed to look up at the young girl. She was cowering near the entrance to an alley, crying. He turned to the man and tried to say something, but the words weren't there, only spit and a croak.

Lyndi stood up and faced the big man. "I'm a police officer. Now, turn around and put your hands up on the wall." She seemed reluctant to draw her badge.

The man began to laugh. "You fine *and* you a copper! Well, fuck you!" He turned and pointed at the woman, "And fuck you!" He turned and pointed at Harry, "And fuck you!" He turned and pointed at the little girl crying at the entrance to the alley, "And fuck you, too!"

That was it. Harry leapt, wedged his shoulder into the man's lower chest and drove him up against the wall. Their hands slapped and grabbed at one another as the man got his footing back and shoved Harry away. Lyndi caught him as he fell back into the street. When the man kept coming to do more damage, Lyndi stepped in front of Harry. She buried her fist into the man's throat and kneed him in the midsection. The man appeared stunned, but kept coming. He grabbed her neck, so Lyndi spun her left arm up and around, and followed it with a right haymaker, again to his throat.

She thought about drawing her snub-nose .32.

She didn't have to. The man was crawling away down the street, fighting for air, the woman following him, suddenly concerned, asking if he was alright. "You must be drunk, she done kicked yer sorry ass."

The little girl wasn't crying anymore. She was following the man and the woman up the street, but walking slowly backward, staring at Harry and Lyndi. Her mother turned and hollered at her, "C'mon, Sharise!" The girl grinned.

"You okay, Harry?" asked Lyndi.

"No, no I'm not. I'm dying."

Lyndi sighed. "Don't worry his balls are in a lot worse shape than yours. Let's just go back to my place. I'll take care of you. Whatya say?"

"Sounds like heaven," said Harry, "sounds like heaven."

CHAPTER TWENTY-FOUR

Come on down to the Yards

"I SAYS MY name's Jebediah Hatch and I live in Back of the Yards and I want to file an assault charge— I mean, uh, I want to press charges on someone who done assaulted me last night out front of my home."

"I understand that, sir," said the uniformed police officer from behind the glass partition. "What is the name of the person you want to file an assault charge against?"

"Well, I don't know his name, but he drive a beat-up silver or gray Camaro and he real tall and big with tattoos, all kinds of racist-like tattoos on himself. Even a damn spider-web tattoo across his bald head and—"

"Okay, well, we can't exactly file an assault charge on someone without a name and an investigation. You can give us a description and we can enter it into our system and go through the investigative process, but we cannot file any assault charges at this point. Do you understand that, sir?"

"But I was assaulted, whipped on my own street." Jebediah's eyes bubbled up and he pointed at the dark bruise on his face. He wanted to turn around, raise up his shirt and show the red streaks across his back but he thought better of it.

"I can have you speak to an officer who can take your statement, and get a description of the man and his vehicle. Were there any witnesses to this incident?"

"Witnesses?"

"Yes, sir, witnesses to the alleged crime that took place."

"Alleged?" Jebediah had grown impatient now. He felt the police officer was patronizing him and he didn't know whether he should mention any witnesses. That might tick some folks off. He didn't think too long on it.

"The head of the Latin Kings was there," he said. "His name is Raymond Delgado. And I, I aint afraid to say it neither. He live just a stone's throw away."

"Was Raymond Delgado the man who assaulted you, sir?"

"No, but he seen it."

The police officer nodded. "Nevertheless, I'm going to have you talk to a member of the Gang Enforcement Unit."

"Gang Enforcement Unit?" Jebediah snickered. The guy wasn't believing him. Fat, lazy pig, just wanted to push him off on someone else.

"Or I can have you fill out a form and you can wait to be contacted by a detective?"

"No," said Jebediah. "I already had to wait just to talk to you."

"Take a seat and someone will be out to talk to you shortly."

Twenty minutes later, a young officer in plain clothes came out to the waiting area and asked Jebediah to follow him back to a desk. Once Jebediah sat down, the officer said, "My name is Dave Flisk and I'm with the Gang Enforcement Unit. So you would like to press assault charges against one Raymond Delgado?"

"Jesus, Mary and Joe!" belted Jebediah. "Hail, no! I don't want to press charges against him, even though he a damn crook and killer and a cockroach—I aint afraid to say it. They was another man—a white man—driving an old Camaro, drove up and we had some words, and he was bigger than me and younger and he took to beating on me pretty severely."

"Where does Raymond Delgado fit into this story?"

Jebediah looked hard at the young cop, his dark hair, his stocky build. His bearded face was long but angular. "I know you from somewhere," said Jebediah. "You patrol the Yards?"

"I'm out and about in the neighborhoods quite a bit. I'm sure we've probably passed on the street or something. Now, tell me about this assault and how Delgado fits into the picture."

"Nah, I seen you somewhere else. Not in the Yards," Jebediah rubbed his chin while peering at the officer. "You been on the television, I think. I watch a lot of television, still got a box, have never bought one of them fancy flat things."

"Let's move on, please, Mr. Hatch. I have work to do."

Jebediah told him the story of the big tatted up guy driving the Camaro, how the guy sucker punched him and then beat him with the belt. He told him how he drew his gun—even produced his FOID card for the officer—but didn't have the guts to pull the trigger. It was a hate crime, he assured officer Flisk, who took diligent notes on the descriptions of the Camaro and of the man, but seemed more interested in the Raymond Delgado portion of the story.

"You say Delgado watched this take place and did nothing in the form of helping you or preventing this man from hurting you any further?"

"No, sir. He did nothin. I'm not sure why he wouldn't neither. An old black man being beat down by a racist white man in the street as a no-good gangbanger looks on." Jebediah sighed. "Come on down to the Yards, man. There aint nobody lookin out for nobody."

"Tell you what we're going to do," said Flisk, "myself and another officer from our unit will pay a visit to your neighborhood."

"And how's that gonna make anything better? You gonna throw Delgado in the can for watchin a man get beat in the street?"

"No, we can't do anything to him for not reporting a crime. It does give us an opportunity to stick our heads in his business and take a look around. You may have heard in the news that he was recently put on probation for a felony charge. Us peeping around, excuse my language, but that usually irritates the shit out of these guys. The fact that we have an excuse to pry helps justify our presence, otherwise we're looked at as if we're harassing without any probable cause. These civil rights groups come down on us and tie up our hands."

"Hail, Delgado and his crew don't give two pennies bout the cops. You guys the least of their worries. What about the big ugly white boy who beat me?"

"Do you think they knew one another or was he in the neighborhood to buy or retaliate—he doesn't exactly fit the profile with the swastika tats and the racist-fueled hate he showed you."

"They all in the neighborhood to buy or kill somebody. But I don't know what he was lookin to do. Dude was evil, though. Could see it in his eyes. They were demon eyes."

"Well, we'll have to talk to one evil dude about another evil dude and go from there. We appreciate you bringing this to our attention today, Mr. Hatch."

CHAPTER TWENTY-FIVE

Do you mind if we take a look around?

FLISK AND OFFICER Boggs parked in front of a two-flat brownstone where Raymond Angel Delgado resided. The property owner was listed as a thirty-seven year old female, likely a relative of Delgado's, Flisk figured.

The neighborhood looked empty of pedestrians except for a man and a woman on the front porch of the two-flat. As Flisk and Boggs exited the car, the two people hurried inside the home and slammed the front door.

"That's not very welcoming," said Boggs.

Both officers were in plain clothes but wearing bullet proof vests, along with their side arms. Boggs rapped on the door.

"What you want?" came a deep voice from behind the door.

"We're sellin girl scout cookies and—"

"Chicago Police Department," interjected Flisk. "We want to talk to Raymond Delgado about an incident that took place up the street."

"Aint nobody by that name live here."

"Open up the door, please. We won't be too long."

"How I know you aint gonna drag me out and beat me? White cops are gunnin blacks in this city. Whose to say you aint lookin to pin-ball a Latino?"

"You know, if you're Raymond Delgado you sure as hell sound like a pussy," said Boggs, who smiled at Flisk but scowled when Flisk didn't smile back.

The door opened and a large man stood there, taking up the entire frame of the door. He was balled and big, looked like a football player. He was the same height as Boggs and the two stood staring at each other.

"You wanna take that vest off and leave your piece in the mailbox? We can go down to the basement and find out who the pussy be."

A few tense seconds past before someone came up behind the large man in the doorway. Flisk recognized him as Edgar Rojas, an associate of Delgado's, the two had been friends since childhood. Rojas had connections in Mexico and was suspected of transporting drugs in and out of the city. "You guys went and pissed off Tiny," he said. The big man took a step out onto the porch, nearly going nose-to-nose with Boggs, who kept his chin up while locking his thumbs in his waistband.

Even though he was sure Rojas knew him from when Delgado was arrested, Flisk felt the need to remind him who he was, "Officer Flisk, this is officer Boggs."

"Yeah, no shit. You bust Delgado, you crash our party and now you want to harass him at his crib? We know you, punk."

"Cool your jets, pal. We just want to ask him some questions about an assault that took place just a few houses up the street a couple nights ago. Are you aware that an assault took place?"

"Man, assaults take place all the time in the Yards. Aint nothin new."

"Make a move limp-dick," said Boggs to the big man named Tiny.

Flisk raised up his hand as if to halt Boggs, then looked at Rojas again, "Is he here?"

Just then a young woman appeared in the doorway behind Edgar. She had long black hair and wore cutoff jean shorts and a black tank-top. "He says he'll talk to them, bro," she said.

A second later, Delgado was at the door, "I don't recall any ass beatin, if that's what you mean. But I'll keep an eye on things for you, you know. Do my part protecting the community."

"Do you mind if we take a look around?" asked Flisk.

"What the fuck you think I'm gonna say to that?"

Boggs turned to Delgado and then peered past him and Rojas at the woman, "C'mon, invite us in to yer crib. Let us see how the top banger of the Kings lives it up. I bet you got plenty of slutty, stanky taco-crotch mommas in there. He pointed past the men at the woman, who was now leaning against the wall in the hallway. "She a tight tortilla?"

The woman flipped him off and the men took a step closer.

"*Mi hermana, ese*," said Rojas, "*Te voy a matar.* I'll kill you."

"Me no speak no español," said Boggs.

"Boggs," grumbled Flisk.

Delgado turned his focus to Flisk. "You don't care bout no old black man gettin his ass kicked in the street. You'd liked to have seen him get a few caps in him. Lay out, bleedin from his face. That's how you cops like it." Delgado pointed directly at Flisk. "That's what you'd rather see, for sure."

Flisk stood silent for a moment, staring, reading him, trying to stay in control, trying to keep his paranoia at bay.

"You know you're not to have any contact or with known gangbangers or be delegating your own gang, right?"

Delgado ignored him.

"How'd it make you feel, shuttin out the lights? Make you feel like you a bad mofo?" Delgado paused. "Good feelin, aint it? A rush?"

Boggs interjected, "What the hell are you talking about? I think you've been using too much of your own H, man. Your brain is fried. Keep it up, homey, and you'll be as stupid as this fat ass." He pointed at the big man named Tiny.

"I'll shit you out my ass," replied the man, his face twisting with tenseness.

"See what I mean?" said Boggs.

"You know, one call to your parole officer and you're in the can," Flisk threatened, again his eyes reading Delgado. "Let's go, Boggs."

"That's right," said the leader of the Latin Kings, waving. "You come around the Yards again, and secrets won't be secrets no more. You know what I mean? I'm tired of your harassment. I better not see your punk ass again."

As they reached the end of the porch the two police officers realized they'd quickly been joined by more members of Delgado's crew. A few men stood around a suped up Oldsmobile Cutlass in the alley next to the two-flat. Another man was sitting on a motorcycle across the street, his right hand hidden by a greasy rag towel draped over his lap. More men loitered on the sidewalk near the building, glancing up at the porch.

By the time Flisk made it back to the cruiser he was sweating profusely. Boggs took one look at him and said, "What's got your panties in a bunch? C'mon, Flisk, you scared of a few beaners?"

"Shut-up, Boggs!" He whispered harshly, pointing and scolding his partner. "Just shut-up!"

CHAPTER TWENTY-SIX

With miles and miles and miles left to go

MY HEAD WAS throbbing so I took my meds and closed my eyes. I fell asleep and had a dream. But when I awoke I couldn't remember any of it. I'm not a poet, but in my groggy and disoriented state, I sat down and wrote this:

Walking through leaves of gold
I can feel the air turning cold
Dreaming of a life unknown
With miles and miles and miles left to go

Man is nothing but a man
No matter the color of his skin
Takes a lifetime to know
Won't you meet me down on Peace Road?

Now the storm's come to stop me in my tracks
Take away all I am
Lay my body in the muddy loam
With miles and miles and miles left to go

All hail the morning sun
But we can't undo what's been done
On the wind our sins blow
Won't you meet me down on Peace Road?

Past the churches and the jails
Hear the choir song and the siren wail
Trying to find my way home
With miles and miles and miles left to go

I come to a ridge with no way around
No way over and no way down
Just a lost and lonely soul
So c'mon won't you meet me down on Peace Road?

Again, I'm not a poet, but something compelled me to write this down. Peace Road is an exit off Interstate Eighty-Eight about an hour west of the city. I spent a lot of time on a farm around there. Life was easy back then. I miss those times.

-**HJW**

CHAPTER TWENTY-SEVEN

When I want to break the rules ...

TINY OPENED THE backdoor of the Durango and carefully eased Alexa out of the SUV.

"Why am I blindfolded, Ray-Ray? What is this about?" she pleaded nervously.

Delgado hurried out of the vehicle, closed the door, and, from behind her, put his hands over the blindfold.

"Why are you doing this?" she asked again, forming a smile to her mouth.

"I want to be sure you are not peeking," he said.

"But where are we?"

"Let me ask you, babe, where do you think you are?"

She fidgeted for a moment, flattening her black dress at her stomach from the billow of a breeze and adjusting her stance in her high-heels. She didn't' worry about whether or not she was revealing too much cleavage.

"It's warm out," she said.

"*Si*. It is summer," Delgado laughed.

"I hear …," Alexa strained to listen, "I hear …"

"What do you hear, babe?"

"It's so quiet, Ray-Ray. Peaceful. Where are we?"

"What is the smell like?" asked Delgado.

She answered quickly, "I don't know. I don't know how to describe it. Nice? Not dirty?"

"*Si*, it is quiet and not dirty smelling," he said as they both laughed. "Babe, you want to get out of the city. Live where the air is clean and the sounds of sirens don't blare all through the night. You want to stop living with your parents, eating their food and abiding by their rules. You want to—"

"When I want to break the rules, I just stay at your place, Ray-Ray," quipped Alexa.

"Well you won't have to anymore, babe. Because this is your new house." He untied the blindfold and hurled it into the air.

Alexa blinked and then went wide-eyed.

It was a mini mansion, complete with two marble columns, large windows and a long winding driveway. She nearly stopped breathing.

"Ray-Ray!" she screamed. "Oh, Ray-Ray!" She hugged him and tried to bunny hop in her heels. "We are going to live here in this mansion? It's beautiful!"

"You, my babe, are going to live here. I pay the rent for you to live here."

"What? I'm going to live in this huge house without you?"

"You can have a girlfriend stay with you when I am not around."

Delgado could see her exuberance quickly dwindle so he escorted her inside the home. "It's got five bedrooms, four baths—one with a Jacuzzi hot tub—a movie theatre room, everything," he said.

The two eventually ended up on the bed in the master bedroom. After making love, she held him tightly. Delgado was already feeling smothered.

"Why do you want me to live here, Ray-Ray?" she said softly into his ear.

"Because I want to know where you are and I want to know that you are safe. We have many enemies, and the cops are snooping around. And you would just be better off here."

"How will you know that if you are not here with me?"

He peeled her arms off of him and sat up. "Because my money is here, too. The basement is off limits to you and your friends."

He stood and dressed. Turning back to her, he said, "That is the one catch in all this for you, babe." He kissed her and went to leave, but she pulled him back down to the bed.

"My brother was right," she said. "And here I thought he was full of it. He's doing stupid things, Ray-Ray. I hope you don't do stupid things, too."

"What does this have to do with you getting to live in a fancy house?"

"A fancy house in the burbs means nothing to me if you're in the Yards getting arrested again by that obsessed cop or shot up in the street by your enemies or bangin hoes like those skanks that fill your flat from time to time," she answered.

And with that Delgado was up and moving out of the room, heading down the spiral stairs.

"Ray-Ray!" She pleaded. "Ray-Ray, I'm sorry! Come have dinner with Edgar and me at my parent's home *manana*! Ray-Ray? *Mi madre* wants to see you! She's making pork carnitas!"

Delgado slammed the front door.

"I am going to tell her about our baby," Alexa said quietly to herself, a tear running down her cheek.

CHAPTER TWENTY-EIGHT

It needs to be equal or noth

LIGHTLY ROCKING IN his chair on the porch, Jebediah thumbed a smear away from the glass of the framed portrait of his wife. He held the picture in his lap and stared at it. "Oh, Adelae, you lucky to be in heaven. You so lucky to be in the kingdom of God. You tell'um for me, Adelae. This world has done gone to hell."

When he looked up toward the street, Jebediah saw an unmarked police cruiser roll up and abruptly park in front of the house. Upon recognizing officer Flisk, he blinked his eyes dry and hid the framed picture behind him. As Flisk approached, Jebediah stood up.

"You catch him? He in the pokey?"

"The what?" asked Flisk, and then ignored the question. "Inside! We need to talk," he said sternly, pointing at the screen door.

"Whatya want with me?" asked Jebediah, stepping toward the door but staring directly into the police officer's eyes.

Flisk stopped, looked down the street nervously and turned back toward Jebediah. His teeth were clinched when he whispered harshly, "Did you sell me out?"

When Jebediah only looked back at him blankly, Flisk commanded, "Inside!"

The two men sat down in a front room, Flisk on the edge of an old couch. He looked anxious, Jebediah noticed, while putting the framed picture down on an end table.

"Did you tell Raymond Delgado who I am?"

Jebediah squinted and then leaned back in his chair and sighed. "Well I'll be, you the cop that shot that kid, the unarmed black kid. Where it be, St. Louis? And wasn't it, yeah, Fisher, officer Fisher. You done changed your name."

"Fuck!" shouted Flisk.

"Now, boy you be watchin your mouth here in this home." He let the young man cool down before asking another question. "Whatya doing still a cop for?"

"Why wouldn't I still be a cop? Did you bother to read a paper after the incident or watch the news? I was never charged with anything—"

"Yeah, but …

"If you didn't say anything to him, then how'd he know?"

"Maybe Delgado just playin mind games with you. Man's a gang-bangin killer, can't be too heavy on brains in the first place. What you think he gonna do anyways, knowin such a thing? He aint exactly sympathetic to the black cause."

Flisk looked up and gave Jebediah a cold stare. "I had over six hundred death threats, had to change my name, move my family to a new city in a new state. They wanted to burn me alive. They wanted to rape and kill my wife," he said quietly. "Goddamn, man, some of the stuff they said on my voicemail, and in emails and whatnot. I knew the minute I saw Delgado's eyes. He didn't have to say anything."

Jebediah raised his eyebrows. "Who do you mean by they?"

"Skumbags. White, black, you name it."

"What you got to worry for? You got a whole police department at your disposal. Gangbangers don't want that kind of attention."

"I can't let the department know my identity's been compromised on account I'll lose my job, be uprooted again, have to start from scratch again. My wife won't stick around. She'll take my baby girl and leave. I gotta take a stand."

Jebediah snickered, "What are you saying, son?"

"I noticed some of his men loitering around my neighborhood yesterday, they weren't lookin for a handout. They were there with the intent to do harm or they were prepping for it. I sent my wife and my daughter off to stay with her parents. She's pissed, but at least they're safe."

"So what you gonna do? Fight Delgado and the Kings? Man, they'll rip the skin from your bones and eat you up like a greasy burrito."

Flisk lowered his head and stared at the carpet. "I gotta send a message or ... or compromise with them."

"Seems you didn't move far enough away if you ask me," said Jebediah.

"Don't you get it?" snapped Flisk, his lip rolling up. "I shouldn't have had to do anything! That kid died—because of the actions of the adults that were around him. He didn't die because of the color of his skin. I didn't pull my gun because they were black. But no matter the evidence, the testimony of witnesses, the grand jury's decision, the attorney general's decision, ignorant people don't want to see it that way."

"Now you callin black people ignorant, son?"

"Does the progress that's been made since the nineteen sixties mean anything?"

"Until you've had to piss in a dirty bucket outside a diner in Mississippi while a white man piss in a clean toilet where it be warm inside, then don't talk to me about how we suppose to feel about progress. Maybe 'progress' aint enough. It needs to be equal or noth."

Flisk nodded. "Maybe it could be, but you'll never want to see it that way. Being the victim has its advantages—"

"Son, you want to talk about ignorance? Well, yer spewing ignorance right here in my livin room."

"Oh, give me a break," said Flisk as he stood up.

Jebediah's voice rose to a yell, "When a white man can beat a black man in the street and all yall cops care to do is bust a gangbanger in the neighborhood, you're sure as shit a race divide still exists in this country! Now get the hail out of my house before I whup your ass!"

Flisk took a deep breath and stood there. He appeared weighed down with exhaustion. Jebediah figured he'd probably been up all night in anticipation of a confrontation with Delgado and his men.

"Look," said Flisk, "you're right, there's still a long way to go. I'm just saying the gap isn't what it used to be and it can only ever be bridged if both sides come to-gether. I'm sorry for coming here." He started for the screen door.

"I reckon they know by now you're in the Yards," Jebediah's voice was low and calm now. It stopped Flisk in his stride. "They got spotters on every corner." He leaned forward, looking hard at the young cop. "You aint scared neither."

"I better leave," Flisk turned toward the door again. Dusk had settled in, shadows spotted the street. He turned back to the old man. "Again, I'm sorry for …"

Jebediah looked away. "Oh hell, I don't know if I would or wouldn't told anyone had I put it together. The evil in this world seems to be makin muck of my mind. Anymore I aint for sure what's wrong and what's right. I just so fed up with it all."

Flisk looked out the screen door and caught the movement of bodies in the shadows. Five, six, seven men, hurrying into a semicircle around Jebediah's front porch. He turned back to the old man.

"They out there, aint they?" calmly asked Jebediah without looking at him.

Flisk nodded anyway.

"And you sure you don't want to call your brethren in blue?"

"I'm gonna get to the cruiser and get out of here," he said, while unholstering his pistol and checking the magazine.

Adelae's picture faced Jebediah, and he looked at it proudly. "No, son," he said as he rose from the chair. "You'll stay in the house. I'm going out there."

"I don't need your help, old man," replied a defiant Flisk. "I don't need anyone to fight my battles."

Jebediah continued to head toward the door. "Well, maybe this here is a chance for us both to help each other." He stopped and turned toward him. "And, I don't need no cop being shot dead on my front porch."

*****

"Go home, boy," said Jebediah, standing on his porch. "Aint nothin for you here."

"You not so wise for being an old man, you know that?" answered Raymond Delgado. "My *hermanos* and I here for some payback that you know nothin about. So you take yourself back inside *viejo* and turn on Wheel of Fortune and send that white boy out here and let us set things straight."

"You let a black man that you've known in this here neighborhood for a long time get whipped in the street by a hatin white man, and you do nothin about it? But when it come to get revenge for one of yer allied gangs on a white cop who shot and killed an unarmed black kid, you suddenly Mr. Righteous? I got news for you, Raymond, you a little pea-brained, dull-witted, inbred PUNK! The only person gettin revenge on anyone is gonna be me on your sorry ass if you don't get off my property. You hear me, lil boy?"

Delgado leapt, bounding up the steps, his men pulling their weapons, ready to follow.

But Delgado never made it to the top step, for he had looked up before he was going to tackle the old man and saw the barrel of a handgun pointed directly at his forehead. He grinned, "You know how to use that?"

Jebediah cocked the hammer back. "I've no qualms bout blowin what little brains you have out the backside of your head."

"The boys shoot you down, leave you leakin blood from all the holes, right here on your own front porch."

"I got no qualms about dying, neither."

Delgado stepped down off the porch. "You know, this is a peaceful Hispanic neighborhood, *viejo*. You in the wrong place. We don't need yer kind here in *Ciudad de Halo*."

"My kind, huh? Shoot, yer dumber than I thought. In the last three years alone theys been more than one hundred fifty people shot in this place you call '*Halo City*.'"

"Yeah?" answered Delgado. "I'd watch yer back. You just wrote your ticket to the grave." He began to walk away.

"We'll see who gets there first," hollered Jebediah. "The line of work you're in, I got my money on you!"

CHAPTER TWENTY-NINE

Say your prayers

THEY PINNED HIS arms behind his back and wrapped his torso in duct tape. They crossed his legs at the ankles and wrapped them as well. All the while, Edgar Rojas was spitting out profanities in both English and Spanish at the men who had barged into his parent's home while they were eating dinner.

Edgar told them he would kill them and their families. And, despite his mother and sister being in the room, he told them he would rape their wives, girlfriends and sisters. And then he told them he would do anything for them if they wouldn't hurt him and his family. And then he pleaded with them to only hurt him, not his mother, father or sister.

"*Somos de Guanajuato!*" he screamed. "*Mi hermana está embarazada!* We are of Guanajuato! My sister is pregnant!"

They knelt his father down in front of him. Edgar Rojas looked past him at his captors and pleaded some more. *"Dinero! Coches rápidos! Putas! Cualquier cosa!"*

"You went up against the wrong people, Rojas. Others need to know that no one goes up against Los Zetas, not in Mexico and not in Chicago. *Diga sus oraciones.* Say your prayers."

Rojas watched as one by one most of his family members were bludgeoned and stabbed to death right before his eyes. His sister was the last to be knelt in front of him.

"Alexa, I'm sorry," he said with tears streaking down his face.

Weeping and holding her stomach, she told her older brother that he wouldn't see any of them in the afterlife. *"Vas al infierno por esto.* You're going to hell for this, Edgar," she said.

The assailants argued over the means of killing her before shooting her dead. No one wanted to stab her.

"Do it!" Hollered Edgar, waiting for his own death.

"No, *Senor.* Your punishment is life. Tell the others. Los Zetas own the city."

CHAPTER THIRTY

Life sorta began here for me

HE HAD JUST made love to her but she was standing in white bikini underwear and he could not take his eyes off of her. Long, firm legs. A core that she had worked hard to keep from going soft. Ample breasts. Tall, the center of her face reaching his chin. Wide, sturdy but delicate looking shoulders. Her long, thin neck. Small but full lips. Her petite nose. Chestnut eyes. A prevalent forehead, proportioned perfect enough to keep her hair from falling into her eyes at all times.

Harry leaned in and planted a weighty kiss in the center of Lyndi's forehead. He took a step back.

Goddamn, Lyndi Carnes, you are something to behold.

"What's up with you, Harry? You're like a lost puppy dog lately. You going soft on me?" She took a step toward him and placed her hand on his chest. She looked up at his eyes, appearing surprised by how intensely he was looking at her. "You up for another round or something, you big stud?"

"Can you just stay the night? Sleep, sleep in my bed …" Harry swallowed hard, fighting back a wave of emotion. "Sleep … in my arms?"

"What the fuck is up with you? I'm serious, now. Tell me what's going on."

He whispered, "I don't know what's going on. I just want you to stay tonight." His face was pleading.

"You sound like a girl, Harry, you know that, right?" They both smiled. "Okay, I'll stay. But you're making me breakfast in the morning, and I don't mean like a bowl of puffs or toast or anything like that. I mean like a big breakfast of eggs, sausages, pancakes—"

"You want me to go out and get you some Krispy Kremes?" he said as they climbed back into his bed.

"No, Harry. I want a grand breakfast."

He slipped his arm beneath her and she rested her head on his chest. After a while, Lyndi looked up and kissed him on the lips. "This is nice," she said and rested her head back down.

This is fleeting, thought Harry.

He knew where he wanted to take her after their big breakfast in the morning. To hell with playing basketball with her guy friends.

I certainly don't need the exercise.

*****

"C'mon, Harry, you're slacking. Cut to the hoop after the pick," hollered Lyndi.

Harry was doubled over, trying desperately to catch his breath, blinking harshly to try to return his vision to clear. "I said I didn't want to fuckin play," he snapped. A silence fell over the gym. Lyndi shot him an irritated look. The other guys looked his way, bewilderment in their faces.

That's great, Harry. You just gave these slow, fat, lazy ass shmoes something to talk about for the rest of the day.

Lyndi tossed him a towel. "How about you sit this one out, let Lyle play?" She gestured toward a fat guy stretching near the sideline. Harry waved her off, disgruntled, but lumbered to the bleachers and sat down.

After he caught his breath and his vision returned, he sat there watching Lyndi. She brought the ball up and crossed over, went between the legs and then fired up a fundamentally-sound jump shot. She was backpedaling before the swish sound.

What an amazing woman. Beautiful. Smart. Sweet. And badass. I've been a lucky man the last year.

"Nice shot, LC!" He hoarsely belted out in an effort to quell the sentimental emotion that was building up.

This was it. It would all be downhill. There would be no more keeping up with Lyndi, no more extreme physical exertion followed by any rewards. The smallest exertion of any kind would be looked at as an accomplishment.

Before it killed him, the brain cancer would no doubt rid him completely of all his physical abilities, not to mention his dignity.

He pushed himself up off the bleachers and stumbled his way to the locker room. Bent over at the sink, he splashed cold water on his face. When he looked up he began to weep. He had seen himself in the mirror as pathetic. It was brief but it was enough to turn the tide. After a minute or two he hurriedly splashed more water on his face and grabbed a towel.

Twenty minutes later Harry emerged from the locker room in regular clothes and all cleaned up. Lyndi had finished her game, showered and was now chatting with a young male trainer at the gym.

"Hey, I was gonna have Brody here go in and see what was taking you so long," she said.

Harry nodded at the young muscled up twenty-something kid, and kept walking.

"Did you chill out in there or not?" asked Lyndi.

He stopped and looked at her. "Can I take you some place now?" His voice sounding desperate.

"Yeah, sure, Harry. Where to?"

*****

It was out where the stretch of interstate was flanked by corn and bean fields on each side that Harry finally said something. "I like the country." He looked at Lyndi and managed a meek smile. It was the first time he had smiled all morning.

"I'm a city girl, Harry," replied Lyndi. "All this space makes me nervous."

"Yeah, but you gotta admit it's peaceful." After a while he glanced up at an overhead sign. Lyndi looked at him curiously. Peace Road next exit, read the sign. He nodded at her.

They left the car near a rundown barn behind an old farmhouse. Harry led her along the high bank of a crick that snaked out to a cluster of thick trees. It was warm and the sun bright, but a light breeze made it comfortable.

"Harry, what is this place? Where are you taking me?"

He briefly turned back, "I want to show you something."

They walked along the side of the crick until they reached the tree line. It took a minute to find the trail, but he took her hand and led her in. The trail had a steep downward slope that led to a shimmering oval-shaped pond. Harry and Lyndi came out of the shadows of the trees on a small outcropping of land overlooking the pond.

"Wow," said Lyndi. "It's beautiful."

"Yeah, in a couple of months it's even more serene. The leaves change colors. It's amazing. How I sorta envision heaven, you know?"

"How do you know about this place, Harry?"

"I grew up here."

"You grew up here? You're from Elburn."

"This was my grandfather's farm. I believe the county owns the land now. Not sure."

Lyndi walked closer to the edge of the landing and looked down, out over the pond. "Seems like a great place for a young kid to go hang out."

"Yeah, life sorta began here for me." The last words of his statement trailed off to a whisper.

"What was that?"

"There used to be a tire tied to a tree around here somewhere and we'd swing out over the water and drop in." Harry looked around for the tree. When he came back to Lyndi she was pulling her top off over her head and then sliding off her shorts, looking at him with a bold grin. She slipped the hairband she had been wearing during basketball from her hair and tossed it to the ground. She stood there for a moment naked in the sunlight. Harry was nearly breathless. She looked like an Angel, streams of light slipping between her limbs. Her hair falling over one shoulder. Eyes, lips, breasts, hips, thighs, legs.

Heaven it is.

He silently told himself that he would try as hard as he could to keep this image in his wrecked brain for as long as possible.

"Just when I thought it couldn't get any more beautiful here, you had to go and do that," he said.

"C'mon, Harry, aren't you gonna go for a dip? Otherwise, why'd you bring me out here?" She leapt from the landing and made a small splash in the water. She was gone, but the image wasn't. He made sure of it, playing it in his head as if she was still standing there.

He stood up and walked over to the edge. As he declothed, he watched her come up for air, pulling her head back so her hair fell over the nape of her neck. He finished undressing as she cleared her eyes of water.

"Lyndi," he said.

"C'mon in, it's nice," she said while treading water and looking up at him.

"Lyndi."

"What is it? You've been acting like you want to tell me something all morning."

"I love you."

"Stop being a pussy and get in the water, Harry." She went under.

Harry looked up at the clear blue sky and then around at the trees.

"Heaven," he said to himself before leaping in.

CHAPTER THIRTY-ONE

I'll get a knife and cut it open

"WHAT YOU DOING in this hood, white girl? You lookin to buy some hooch, you hit the corner, yo."

The woman ignored the group of men. "Got a delivery for the general at this here building."

"Who callin, yo?"

"Duante, from Duante's Meats on twenty-seventh," she pretended to look bewildered. "What, you don't know Duante, the butcher? Best cuts in Chicago. No? Well, he must know you guys cause he told me to deliver this. Ribeyes, strips, tenderloins, T-bones, filets, courtesy of Duante, the butcher."

"Damn straight, yo!" the man got up from the stoop, a silver semi-automatic pistol in his waistband, and began to walk over to where the woman had set down the cooler.

Another man, shirtless, also sitting on the stoop, looked up suspiciously at the woman. He looked her over and darted his eyes to the other young man. "Wait, Lil Zero, aint Duante's Meats in Black Cobra country?"

"I don't give a shit where it came from, yo. It's fresh meat. Go stoke Granny's grill out back. It got some petro still in it. Let's have us a feast!"

"Cooler needs to go to Big Frank, fellas, or I'll get my ass fired," said the woman. "And I need this job, got three kids to feed, one with special needs. Can't feed kids with no money, you know?"

"Them big tits feed a village," snapped Little Zero. The other men on the porch laughed.

The shirtless man laughed, too, then said, "She about to have three more right fuckin now!"

More laughter.

Another man quipped, "Hey, big Bertha, I got some special needs!" And cupped his crotch.

More laughter.

"Can yall just make sure the meat gets to Big Frank," said the woman. She started back to the curb where she had parked an old, gray Camaro.

"Hey, fat white bitch," hollered Little Zero to more laughter, "why's the damn cooler all duct taped, yo?"

"To keep it fresh, YO!" said the woman defiantly. She got into the Camaro and drove off.

*****

The cooler, with its dirty white lid, scuffed-up blue sides and gray duct tape wrapped firmly around it, sat on the floor of the porch, the men staring at it.

"You best carry it on in to Frank, Lil Z," said the shirtless man. "He sees you out back chawin on a ribeye, he's gonna grill one yer bones up. And get that damn piece out of plain sight! Five-O do a drive by and see you carryin, they'll case the house, pinch Frank and run us up to county!"

"Yo, don't I know that? I got it." Little Zero tucked the gun further down into his waist. "But you heard the boss man, we gotta keep our eyes open, yo, muthafuckin gangbangers droppin like flies these days. Boss man said we be expandin our operations soon, and I got dibs on the Forty-Second Street corridor, yo!"

"You get into that, Two-Sixers light you up."

"They ain't got no leader. They had to *scrape* The Scraper out of the backseat of his own car!"

The men laughed in unison as Little Zero hefted the cooler up into his arms. "Yo, now, I bet boss man gonna dole out some corners tonight and I bet he gonna let us all eat like kings."

*****

Big Frank Beaumont, head of the Black P Stones, stood over a table counting cash. He carefully bundled up twenties in thousand dollar stacks and placed them among the others on the table. A window air-conditioner hummed at one end of the living room and Beaumont had the television turned up loud, a re-run of The Cosby Show blaring from the set—season eight, "Cliff gets jilted," episode.

Beaumont snickered at the irony.

Little Zero entered the room carrying the cooler and dropped it down on the floor.

"That thing better be filled with bills, Lil Z," said Beaumont. "I already got an A/C brought in, don't need no ice."

"It's somethin better, boss man. Yo, it's fresh meat from a butcher."

"Who? What butcher? Who paid for it?"

"Aint no one had to pay for it. It's free, yo. T-bones, filets and whatnot."

Beaumont stopped counting and put down the stack of cash. He stared at the cooler.

At thirty-two years old, Frank Beaumont wasn't considered young in the gang scene. Bullet holes and knife scars told the story of a rough career making it on the streets. He'd been in jail a few times for petty offenses and heard stories.

Little Zero broke the silence. "I'll get a knife and cut it open."

"Italians were good at that shit," Beaumont finally spoke. "Send a package to a man. He open it and get his face blown off right in his own house, in his own kitchen. That's some serious shit, makin bombs."

"Yo, you think there's a bomb in the cooler, boss? Like, a real bomb?" Little Z looked worried, his upper lip curling and his eyebrows popping up.

"Mexican cartel started using bombs, too. Do more damage," Beaumont continued to mumble, staring at the cooler. "Could be, Lil Z. Get a broomstick. Tape a sharp knife to it. Take it and the cooler down into the cellar. Open the thing from a distance and if we don't here an explosion, we'll know you aint plastered all over the damn walls."

Little Zero's right hand began to tremble. "Why I don't take it outside and try to open it, yo?"

"Cause if it blows your nuts off outside, dumbass, the goddamn cops show up. If it blows your nuts off in the cellar, then I blow your brains out in the cellar and just pack up and move on out of this shit hole. Now, get to it! And if yer still in one piece after this, don't ever bring me a cooler or a package or nothin that you haven't already opened!"

Carefully, Little Zero carried the cooler down into the cellar. He came back up, found a broomstick and taped a knife to it, then headed back downstairs.

"Shut the goddamn door!" Hollered Beaumont.

After twenty minutes or so of trying to cut the duct tape from a distance with the broomstick, Little Zero tossed it angrily into the corner of the cellar. He sat on the step looking at the cooler, wiping the sweat from his forehead, breathing in the stale smell of the basement.

Finally he said, "Fuck it," and gaited over to the broomstick, ripped the knife off the end and went about slashing the duct tape off the cooler.

When he was finished, he took a deep breath, closed his eyes, grabbed his crotch and yanked open the lid. He opened his eyes and smiled and then closed the lid just as swiftly as he had opened it.

No explosion. Nothing but ice. "Yo!" he screamed, and hefted the cooler up into his arms, hurrying up the stairs.

"Yo, boss man, I still here," he hollered excitedly. "I got dibs on a T-bone, yo!"

He put it down in front of Beaumont, who was smiling now, back to counting his cash. "Still got your balls, boy? Well, I'll be."

Little Zero called in the other men from out on the porch. Opening up the cooler he took a step back, his arms up and wide as if he had brought his master a treasure to behold.

The smell was instantly nauseating, a wave of dead fish. Beaumont noticed the piece of paper taped to the inside of the lid, YOU'RE NEXT," it read in big black bold letters.

He got up and moved over to the cooler.

"What the fuck?" he said, while swiping a layer of ice off the top and revealing two limbs—the stumps with bone and frozen flesh sticking out. He put his hand over his mouth, gagging. "Holy hell!" The other men grimaced and briefly turned away.

Beaumont noticed it first, the Black Cobras tattoo. It was on one of the arms, the snake's head rising up with fangs and a split tongue, the rest of its body coiled underneath. And the name at the bottom: "Roundtree."

"Jesus! It's Lionel Roundtree's body all cut up in my livin room! Who brought this to me? Get this thing outta here! Wait! Shit!"

He grabbed Little Zero by the collar and shoved him against a wall. "You think this is funny? You think this is a joke? You tryin to make me laugh? I'll put two bullets in both your eyes!"

"No, boss, some fat white bitch brought it up here," Little Zero pleaded. "Said it was free meat courtesy of someone named Duante … Duante, the butcher."

Beaumont turned his attention back to the cooler and then peered around at his men. "Jesus, we gotta get this outta here. Go dump it somewhere. No! Wait till dark, no one sees you!"

"Yo, can I close the lid, boss?" asked Little Zero.

CHAPTER THIRTY-TWO

Just life

EVER SINCE MY grandfather died on a crisp fall day had I wanted to die in autumn.

A farmer, Joseph Everett West lived off Peace Road in DeKalb County, not far from where I grew up. The farm, nearly three hundred acres, had a crick that ran directly through it and a large pond that butted up against its outer most point. The pond was surrounded by forestry, tall, thick red, sugar and Japanese maples. There was room to walk the crick all the way down to the pond. And that's what I recall doing the most as a kid, running my ass off down along the muddy banks of that crick until I reached the pond where a tire hung from a tree. I'd swing out over the water and drop right in. Swim out and do it again. And again. And again. I never even considered how precious life was. Just remained focused on how far I could swing out and drop in. Sometimes I'd cannonball. Sometimes I'd flip. Sometimes I'd just release and let gravity drop me whichever way.

During high school on Friday or Saturday nights some friends and I would go out there to drink beer, talk about girls and about how much money we were going to make when we got older. Over the years, I took more than a few girlfriends out there, too. Hot summer nights, our bare skin lit by a pale moon, skinny dipping. No cares, no worries, no concerns. Just life.

After grandpa's funeral years ago I walked the crick for what I figured would be the last time. Strolled on down to the water's edge. It was late afternoon in October, a gentle cool breeze and the hue of a gloaming high in the sky. I didn't worry about who owned the farm at that point. The small-framed farmhouse and the corrugated sheds where the equipment was once stored were a good distance from the pond. But I took in the leaves—red, gold, and bright yellow on the ground, floating in the air, on the water. They surrounded the pond tethered to thick limbs. The tire was gone, probably stuck in a foot of muck at the bottom of the pond. A portion of the rope, worn and tattered, swung on the breeze.

It's a good season to die in, autumn. Transformation in the air. I told myself back then, that's when I'd like to go, fall with the leaves. But I had caveats. I wanted to die old, though with my faculties well intact. In other words, I wanted to be present. To know. To welcome it. To be at peace with it.

Grandpa was never at peace. He died without making amends with my father. They never saw eye to eye to begin with, but they rarely spoke after dad met, fell in love with and eloped to Vegas with mom while they were both attending college at Northern Illinois University. A messed up situation considering my father never ended up too far away from the farm.

When dad would invite him over, grandpa always had somewhere to go or something to do. He didn't seem to have a problem with me though. I always listened attentively to his advice, his instructions, his opinions, his ramblings. I never judged him or criticized his views. Just listened. Later, I gathered, grandpa was proud of who I was and who I became, though he never showed such emotion.

He died of dementia, not knowing that mom, god bless her, visited and read to him and helped him eat while in hospice care. She told me that near the end he once mumbled to her, "You're an Angel, an Angel … that done fell in an oil well." She had laughed she told me, and then replied, "Ah, I wish it had been a big vat of chocolate, Joseph."

Mom was a looker. I once showed Lyndi a photo of Beatrice as a young woman and Lyndi commented that she looked a lot like the beautiful actress Halle Berry. I heard a lot of such compliments about my mother growing up. She was beautiful and smart, was going to be a teacher or a professor at a university. Instead, she married my father young, had a kid, and settled into a life as a homemaker in a small predominantly white town in the Midwest.

The two of them once told me they used to drive down to Tennessee to visit her family every once in a while, but dad eventually grew to loathe the trips. While Beatrice's mother took a liking to him and welcomed him with her stout open arms and her scrumptious home-cooking, my mother's father and her brothers were a different story. Mom told me that dad was never really embraced by them. By the time I came along, I think we went to Tennessee maybe three or four times is all. Too bad, I liked the rolling hills of Tennessee. The trees leading up the Great Smoky Mountains flourished in autumn.

Autumn: a good time to die. Transformation.

Seems too conventional to die in winter.

-HJW

CHAPTER THIRTY-THREE

Don't come any closer

THE LAWN WAS nearly knee-high in length, the windows closed despite the breezy summer day and the drapes drawn. Rolled up newspapers were strewn across the front porch and the mailbox overflowed with bills.

The house needs some love, thought Lyndi, as she strolled up the steps of Harry's small bungalow. She looked at the mailbox and the newspapers again.

Harry had a lot on his plate. Maybe he took that trip somewhere alone.

He didn't need to tell her he was going to go by himself. He could do what he wanted. She had been too busy with the gang murders to connect with him over the last few weeks. She hadn't received a call from him either, figured he was enjoying his time away from the grind of being a public defender for so many years.

Either that or he was busy looking for a job. What the hell, she'd stop by today, try to clear her head of work.

Maybe Harry was feeling frisky and wanted to clear his head, too.

After locating the hide-a-key rock Harry kept in a planter near the door, she went in and called out his name. A whiff of stuffy air met her in the foyer. It was eerily quiet. Harry was usually always bustling around his place, fixing this or that or sweeping the floors or cooking or busting out some pushups. He was always doing something when she came over. It was one of the things that attracted her to him. He seemed to try to do his best to keep up with her energy.

She made her way up the stairs, calling his name again.

Maybe it was, Hawaii, here I come without LC, she thought, momentarily regretful of turning down the invite.

She had figured he was simply caught up in the moment. A few games of basketball, a drive out to the country. Some frolicking in a pond on property his family used to own. She had sat in his arms overlooking the water when he mentioned wanting the two of them to take off for someplace exotic for a week or more. She remembered she had laughed at the suggestion and it seemed to irritate him. He had been quiet on the ride back to Chicago.

The bedroom was dark, a scattered mess of clothes, towels and trash. She said his name in a serious manner this time, unbuckled the strap on her holster and rested her hand on the grip of the gun. The room looked foreign to her. Harry was a stickler for organization and cleanliness. It was her who had no desire to keep things tidy.

As she slowly entered the room, she heard a faint voice. "Don't come any closer."

Harry's gaunt face settled into a pillow, the rest of him under thick covers on the bed. His face was covered in facial hair—a smidge of grayness on the corner of one side of his chin—but she could make out sharp cheekbones and a dullness in his eyes. She immediately took her hand off her gun.

"Harry, what's going on? You look like hell."

"Stay there. You don't want to catch this … nasty flu virus," he choked out a cough.

Lyndi noticed prescription meds on the nightstand, three bottles next to each other. She began to step into the room—

"No, Lyndi! I need … I need to rest. I just need to sleep this damn thing off. Okay? Call you tomorrow."

She stared at him for a moment. "How long have you been like this, Harry?"

"Couple uhva … uhva days is all," he stammered. "I'll be fine. It's the lizzy, lousy flu bug. Call you in a day or two."

"You need anything?"

He didn't answer, only closed his eyes. Lyndi thought there may have been an answer coming but he didn't want to make the effort.

"Are you sure, Harry?" she asked sternly.

He did not open his eyes, only replied, "Goodbye, LC."

She listened to him snore briefly before returning to her car.

He can take care of himself. He's not a child. And I'm not a woman who takes care of men.

CHAPTER THIRTY-FOUR

It's your lucky night

THE FUZZINESS FROM the three whiskey sours was dissipating, but Mike Coughlin's emotions were not. He gripped the steering wheel of his Lexus tighter and exhaled an angry sigh. He didn't care that he hadn't changed clothes, still in one of his Dolce and Gabbana tailored suits, still in his fancy Salvatore Ferragamo wing-tip dress shoes. He didn't care about anything.

He had plenty of cash on him, a briefcase full sitting in the passenger seat.

What if it's not enough?

The drive into the city was quicker than usual. No stop-and-go traffic at one o'clock in the morning. Not on this night. Interstate Eighty-Eight rolled and the Eisenhower Expressway hummed. He had left his mansion in Naperville with his wife, Nancy, fast asleep. She wouldn't wake up and see him missing anyway, not with the Trazodone the doctor put her on to help her sleep off the pain. She was a wreck. She hadn't stopped sobbing for the last few weeks. Hadn't eaten anything either. She'd drank plenty of wine but it wasn't numbing anything.

She'll never get over it. We'll never get over it.

Mikey, or Michael Aaron Coughlin Jr., the couple's only child, was a good kid. Smart, athletic and handsome. Blond hair, blue eyes, a svelte, muscular body as he grew into his teen years, and a charming personality. Starting pitcher on the high school baseball team, just like his father had been. And just like his father had done, he was hoping to walk-on at Notre Dame next year. An athletic scholarship wasn't necessary, Mike had explained to the coaches during a visit to the university. "Save it for some kid who needs it," he told them proudly. "I'll pay the school to put him on the team, donate a wing, whatever it takes."

Mikey will never play baseball for Notre Dame. Never go to college. Never get married, have children. The thought of this angered his father more. He wiped tears from the corners of his eyes, and pressed down on the gas pedal.

The officer from the Gang Enforcement Unit had said to exit off California. Head south. Turn left at Pershing to juke up to Ashland and south again. *El Naranjo*, a little store, fruits and vegetables.

It'll be open at this hour?

Of course, it's a front. The drug business never closes.

He pulled into the parking lot and watched a group of men, many of them drinking from either cans or bottles in brown paper bags, eye his Lexus. Coughlin hurried into the store. Indiscreetly, he marched up to the clerk,

156

pulled out a wad of cash, and said, "Night Train, I'm here for Night Train."

The young man looked up from a smut magazine and replied, "We don't sell Night Train here. We aint no liquor store."

"Johnny fuckin Ayalla. You know what I mean, you little spic," said Coughlin, surprising himself. "You're the CI officer Flisk told me to—" He shot a look out at the parking lot. Some guys from the corner had now meandered over near the Lexus.

"You keep your mouth shut," whispered the young man, harshly. "You not only get me killed, but yerself, too. I don't make it look on the level, then they pop me when I leave the store and rob the shit out of your sorry ass. Now, go get a basket of some fruits and veggies, and make it look real."

"What?"

"Cantelope, asparagus, whatever the fuck!"

Mikey loved strawberries, thought Coughlin, staring down at a stand full of the fruit. He jammed his hand into the pile of red and took a handful, tossing them into the basket while looking back up at the clerk with hostility. He didn't care about buying fucking fruits or vegetables in the late hours in this shitty Chicago ghetto.

He dropped the basket on the counter and peeled off five one hundred dollar bills from his wad of cash.

"Another five bones. This line of strawberries are trucked in from California," said the young man. "Throw in an extra five bones and I won't let the boys out there car-jack you."

Reluctantly, Coughlin peeled off more bills from his wad.

"Take Damon down to Seventieth Place—not Seventieth Street—but Place, turn right. Second adobe in on the right. They'll be soldiers on the corner and on his stoop, and they'll see you comin from a mile away. But good luck anyway, you know."

"Fuck off," said Coughlin. He grabbed the basket and walked out.

You got the balls to do something, now's the time to do it, he remembered the officer saying. They were at the spot where the police had found Mikey's Mustang, or what was left of it. The jackers had done a number on it, probably raced it down in the tunnels of Lower Wacker, before leaving it in a heap of crumpled and smoking metal.

Maybe Mikey just gave it to them, so doped up.

No. He loved that car. Took real good care of it.

Flisk. Officer Flisk. Probably felt bad for me. Saw the pain in my eyes. Said he'd do it for cheap. No way. It's my son. I'll avenge him. Maybe it's a man's thing. Won't change things, but it might make living with it a little easier. Who knows?

But he was right. Why the dealer? Just a little piss-ant taking orders. Why not the leader of the gang that the dealer was selling for? A face-to-face with the devil himself?

As the streetlights whipped by, Coughlin thought about the night they found Mikey doped through the bones in an abandoned house on the south side. The cops flat-out told him his body was in rigor mortis.

I'm the one who asked the stupid question, "Are you sure he's dead?"

Coughlin figured his son had tried drugs, but he didn't think it was serious drugs like heroin or cocaine.

Why didn't he talk to me? I just never saw it coming. I never saw anything, never around. At the office, on a work trip, at the country club. Horrible father. Horrible.

He opened up the center console and grabbed the fifth of Jack Daniels. He took a hit, forced it down, and then another.

What are you doing, Mike? You don't know what you're doing. You don't have a gun. What the fuck are you doing in the ghetto this late with a briefcase of cash? What do you hope to accomplish here?

Coughlin slammed on the brakes to avoid running into men that had seemed to just appear in the street. He hadn't realized he was now in a neighborhood. The men looked Mexican, maybe three or four of them, loitering. A couple wore doo-rags on their heads. One took a pistol from his waistband and pointed it at Coughlin through the windshield.

"Game time," he said to himself.

He got out of the car slowly but confidently. "It's your lucky night."

"Yer damn right it is, asshole. You in the wrong hood, man. But I like that ride."

"I got something worth more than the car. I need you to let me go on my way down the street, pay a visit to your boss and for you to pretend I was never here."

The men looked stunned. "And why we let you do that?" asked the man with the gun.

"Fifty thousand dollars in cash in this here briefcase," Coughlin lifted the case up and put it on top of the car.

The man with the gun walked closer, grinning. "You stupid, man." The three men around him began to laugh. "I just shoot you in the face, bitch. Then, take your money."

"Then you won't get another fifty thousand in cash delivered to you in the parking lot of that filth hole *El Naranjo*, the fruit and vegetables place, tomorrow night."

"Fuck you."

"And another fifty the next night."

"Fuck me. Now, you're full of shit."

"Shoot me then. Take this money, go blow it on your gold chains, your tattoos, your chinos, and your ho's and be right back in the ghetto in a week. *OR*, become very wealthy men in a week's time."

Another man jumped in, "You gonna pay us the fifty every night for seven nights?"

"Five nights, *amigo*," said Coughlin, holding up his hand. "A quarter of a million dollars." Coughlin could sense the men were either trying to do the math in their heads or trying to decide who they were going to kill of the other three to come away with more of the loot. The more he watched them contemplating, he figured it was the latter.

"What you wanna see Night Train for?"

"Got some business with him. You fellas agree to this then the stipulations to get the full amount are as follows: You never saw me or my car, no matter what happens in that house."

The man with the gun lowered it. "That it?"

Coughlin nodded. "Let me through, go up to the house. Call the hounds off the porch if they're up there."

"I give you a key to the front door."

Coughlin nodded. "That would be helpful, thank you."

"You got a piece?"

He didn't answer.

The man smiled back at him.

"I can surmise that you're an intelligent man," said Coughlin. "I don't make it out, there won't be any more money for you other than this fifty grand." Coughlin tossed the briefcase to the man, who looked in it and nodded. The man then gave a knowing sign to the other three.

"Wait here," he said to Coughlin.

One of the men came around to where Coughlin was standing, walked past him and got into the driver's side seat of the Lexus. He said, "It is a real nice ride."

Coughlin watched the other two men walk back to the house with the briefcase.

I'm a dead man. They're going to rat me out and this Johnny Ayalla is going to kill me.

Fifteen minutes later the two men returned. "Night Train is tied up right now," said the man who had pulled the gun earlier. The other men laughed. "He's really tied up and he's all yours, *amigo*. We'll see you tomorrow night. You don't show, we'll find you and tie *you* up."

Coughlin let out a breath.

The man continued, "But, *amigo*, Johnny Night Train Ayalla is one bad motherfucker. Luckily, he was asleep for us. He's gonna be pissed. And we gotta protect our investment. So I recommend you take a piece in with you." The man turned his gun around so the handle was pointing at Coughlin.

Peering into the back of the Lexus, Coughlin saw his son's baseball equipment. He had gotten it out of the wrecked Mustang on the night the cops found the car. He looked at the metal, big barreled bat sitting atop the bag, and then back at the man.

"No, I'm good," he said.

CHAPTER THIRTY-FIVE

Life is not easy

SUICIDE, IN THE traditional sense, was never an option. I didn't have the guts. I didn't want to lay that burden on Lyndi—the whole "Why did he do it?" thing. I didn't want to mess anyone else up. Obviously, I was messed up. The disease had screwed with my thought process.

Life is not easy. In the short time you're here, you want to make a difference. Sure, I was scared to die, but I was more in fear of failing. I had to do something drastic just to let go. There were times I felt I was trying to swim to the surface and someone was tugging on my ankles. I needed a reason to keep fighting, even though by the end of the round I'd be permanently knocked out for good.

My work was not enough. My personal life was not enough. The sun was not enough. The blue sky was not enough. Laughter wasn't enough. Friends weren't enough.

When the tasting, the smelling, and the seeing began to fade and the amount of seizures increased, I knew it was only a matter of time.

Lyndi was always enough, but as the symptoms worsened I couldn't let her get close. I texted her that I had recovered from the "flu bug" but that I needed some space, some time to get my life on track, find out what I wanted to do and what I felt the future held for me. I hinted about us not being on the same page about our relationship. She knew I wanted to marry her, and that I wanted children.

I could have gone the sensitive route of, "Due to the deadly racial tensions in the city, I think it's a good idea we stay away from each other for a while," but Lyndi would have seen right through that bullshit. I had to be straight with her.

I did mention that it was probably a good time for her as well, with the city steeped in chaos. It was likely to get worse before it got any better. I knew her job was probably more demanding than ever, but, of course, she'd never show it.

It wasn't difficult to fake breaking up with Lyndi Carnes but she was true to herself when she replied back, "You're a pussy for doing this via text. Take care, Harry. LC."

Lyndi Carnes didn't suffer from heartbreak. She did the heartbreaking. It was only a matter of time before she'd invite me out for a drink and drop the, "This thing has run its course," line.

The text wasn't couth, I'll admit. But I couldn't let her see the way I was quickly deteriorating. As I put down the phone, I prayed that whatever supreme spirit exists that it would grant me a last wish of seeing her image in my mind before the end.

I felt I was owed that.

-HJW

CHAPTER THIRTY-SIX

A shell of a man

THE ONLY THING Raymond Delgado could think to say to his friend was, "How are you holding up?"

Edgar Rojas sat there still, his head tilted downward. Delgado realized his friend couldn't look him in the eye. He wanted to tell him that the tragedy had given him sleepless nights. That he hadn't eaten much. Hadn't wanted to party lately. Delgado wanted to tell him that it had forced him to do some soul searching. But it didn't seem appropriate to complain about such things, considering what Edgar had been going through.

"Look at me, Edgar," Delgado insisted.

When he lifted his head Delgado saw the empty void in his eyes. A shell of a man. *Un zombi.*

"You have given up nothing to the police?"

The zombie nodded.

"You want to go home?"

When Rojas only stared at him blankly, it unnerved Delgado. "What do you want?"

"*Nada*," whispered Rojas harshly as a flood of tears streamed down his face. "*No quiero nada.* It's you who should want something."

"What should I want, Edgar?" asked Delgado. "I want your family back. I want what you want. I'm sickened by this. This is not what we—"

"You cannot run from them!" Edgar said as he stood and leaned over the table, shaking his head and wiping his face dry with his hand. "If they want you dead, they will kill you. I'm sorry, *amigo*. I should never have gotten you into this."

"But you said we have *protección*!"

"We have nothing, *amigo*!" Edgar shouted. "What does protection give me now? I am fatherless. I am motherless. They will slice you up," he twirled around to members of Delgado's crew standing against the wall, "and the rest of you! They will stop at nothing!"

Delgado tried to calm Edgar by putting out his hand. "You know what the Sinaloas are capable of. They will send someone."

"*El Chapo* could break from prison again and again and all the Sinaloas could come up here and it wouldn't make a difference."

"Edgar! What are you telling me here?"

"They are not going to bother with who done this to *mi familia*. I, you, mean nothing to them. All they want is the turf, *el Mercado*. They want to move product in and out of Chicago. They just gonna bring hurt and sorrow. You'll soon be swimmin in another blood bath. It aint worth it, *amigo*. You will lose everything."

Delgado opened up his arms, "I have nothing, Edgar."

"No, *amigo*. It is I who have nothing." Edgar turned away and began to weep again. *"Mi hermana estaba con bebé."*

The blood drained from Delgado's face and he fought to hold in his emotions. Angrily, he dismissed members of his crew but told Tiny to wait by the door. He stood and walked over to Edgar. "Tiny will drive you over to the Hinsdale stash house and you will take one hundred K and then you will go far away. Up north, out east, I don't care where, but you never come back and you never speak of this. You hear me, Edgar?"

Edgar spit out the words frantically. "I am going. I am done. I don't want any part of this no more. I wish I'd never been born." He looked up. "I'm sorry I got you mixed up in all this. I should never have gotten involved with them."

"You had no choice," replied Delgado. "They would not have given you a choice."

"You should get out, too. Ray," Edgar reached over and put his hand on Delgado's arm. "I know she didn't mean anything to you. I know she was just a stupid *puta* but —"

"Shut-up, Edgar!" snapped Delgado, shoving his hand away. "Don't say such things about the dead!" He pointed for his grief-stricken friend to immediately leave the room.

Once Rojas had turned his back to him, Delgado nodded to Tiny. It was a slight gesture, but Delgado had ordered the death of his life-long friend.

Before Rojas had arrived at the two-flat, Delgado had worked it out what Tiny was to do if his boss gave him the nod. He was to take Rojas to the Hinsdale stash house and kill him in the basement. Tiny was to wait there until Delgado arrived so he could help dispose of the body.

Delgado didn't want to go along for the actual killing. There had been too much death lately. Everything was happening too fast. He needed a moment to grieve and then gather himself.

He sat down and dropped his head into his hands, bawling like a child.

CHAPTER THIRTY-SEVEN

At least seventy-five gangs

News Report

FBI being consulted as murders of gang leaders reaches double digits

City on edge with recent killing in Columbus Park

IN WHAT HAS now become national news, another leader of one of Chicago's most notorious gangs was found bludgeoned to death in a parking lot in Columbus Park last night.

The killing of Lonnie Banks, 27, originally of Norridge, brings the number of gang leaders murdered in the city to ten in the last few months. Chicago police officials say the FBI is being consulted on the pretense that the killings are serial related and therefore reside in the bureau's jurisdiction. Although a turf war has been ongoing for years between many of the city's most prominent gangs, representatives and police informants insist the high-profile murders are not being carried out by any sole faction, according to a top police official who asked to remain anonymous because he is not authorized to speak publically about the case.

The police official also confirmed that the possible motive could include vigilante justice by private citizens or the killings could be orchestrated by the Mexican cartel, which has been mentioned as a possibility in the family murdered recently in Gage Park.

"We're investigating all possibilities at this point," he said. "With the amount of media exposure this has drawn, there's a chance that some of the murders may be copycat related, ordinary citizens fed up with the gang activity in their neighborhoods taking the law into their own hands at the most opportune time."

A lack of witnesses and cooperation from citizens has caused frustration for the officials investigating each murder, said the source.

One murder in particular, that of Fernando "El Demonio" Batista, 29, thought to be the leader of the Latin Pachucos, has been particularly vexing, according to the police official. Batista's torso was found in a basement beneath the rubble of a rowhouse on the 800 block of Kedzie after the building burned to the ground during the early morning hours of Sept. 12.

Despite the building's location in a well-populated residential area, the emergency response department did not receive a call into its 911 center until well after the structure had been completely destroyed. Authorities found no evidence that the rest of Bautista's body was burned in the fire.

Another obstacle hampering the overall investigation, said the police official, has been the dozen or so false confessions in the last few weeks.

"These guys come in and confess because they want to get their fifteen seconds of fame. It takes up our time tracking down these futile leads, but we can't rule any-thing out."

It happened to be a group of kids playing basketball in Columbus Park that came upon the body of Banks, said to be the leader of the Four Corner Hustlers. The coroner's office said Banks was killed by blunt force trauma to his head. He was found in the backseat of a Chevy Monte Carlo.

An audit last year by the Chicago Police Department revealed that the city has at least seventy-five gangs with six hundred and twenty-five factions.

The following is a list of the gang leaders murdered in the city in the last few months:

Joseph "Killer Joe" Elston, Black Disciples. Found shot to death with two associates in a car at 49th and Winchester on June 14.

Simon "The Scraper" Gutierrez, Two-Six Gang. Found shot and stabbed to death with two associates in a vestibule on 16th Street and Laramie on June 14.

Quentin "Q" Rollins, Outlaw Bloods, shot at point blank range in a massage parlor on Cullerton and West-ern avenues on July 2. Although others were in the build-ing, no one claimed to have witnessed the incident.

Darvin "DC" Cochrane, Insane Popes (South Side), found with associates riddled with bullets in Washington Park on Aug. 18.

Lionel Roundtree, Black Cobras. His body parts were found stuffed in a cooler in a vacant lot near the

1400 block of 66th Street on Aug. 27. Police officials be-lieve the murder weapon to be a chainsaw.

Frank Beaumont, Black P Stones, shot multiple times in the face, throat and torso at close range on the corner of 52nd & Loomis on Sept. 8.

Fernando "El Demonio" Bautista, Latin Pachucos. Bastista's torso was found under debris after a fire in a rowhouse on the 800 block of Kedzie in Humboldt Park on Sept. 12.

Johnny "Night Train" Ayalla, Chicago Imperial Gangsters, bludgeoned to death in a home in the 400 block of Seventieth Place in West Englewood on the early morning of Sept. 17.

Buford Bales, The Vice Lords, found floating in the Chicago River south of Eighteenth Street on Sept. 20. He was bludgeoned before being drowned.

Lonnie Banks, Four Corner Hustlers, found bludg-eoned to death in the backseat of his car in Columbus Park on Sept. 25.

CHAPTER THIRTY-EIGHT

I can't seem to love

THE FOG EASED off the dead calm lake. Lyndi could see a man sitting up near the bow of the little boat. She reeled in her line and put her fishing rod down.

"Dad?"

The man, chewing on an unlit cigar, turned to her. He kept his fishing rod straight off the bow of the boat. "What is it, Lyndi Sue?"

"What are you doing here?"

"I'm not here."

She studied him, confused. "Why did you leave me?"

"For country, sweetheart. To protect the country. To protect what's in it. Life and liberty. To protect you. That's why I left."

"What if I was a boy and your son? Would you have left a son?"

"Yes. If duty called, I would have left a son."

As he started to turn back toward his rod again, she called out, "I can't seem to love."

He turned and faced her again. "Well, I'm not exactly the person you should get advice on love from, but I'd suggest letting your guard down some. Open up. It's okay to be vulnerable. Follow your heart. If it feels like love then it must be love." He took the cigar from his mouth and chuckled. "Now don't I sound like a goddamn Hallmark card?" He put the cigar back into his mouth. "The funny thing about you Lyndi Sue is that you're not afraid to love, you're just not sure if love is a real thing or not."

"I shouldn't be blaming you for that."

"It's alright. I'm probably to blame. But I've never known how to express love, which doesn't mean I don't believe in it. I do know I love you, Lyndi Sue."

"Why are you saying all the right things to me?"

He turned to tend to his fishing rod again. "Because you're dreaming," he said.

CHAPTER THIRTY-NINE

The hate crime

EARLY ONE MONDAY morning, as more Chicago police officers filed into the room—some in plainclothes, some in standard uniforms, others, commanders, in dress blues—Lyndi reflected on the last few months: A white cop shoots a black kid in the street. Two dead gang leaders on the same night. Another murdered gang leader found weeks later. Eight more murdered in the span of a few weeks.

It had been an exhausting summer. Along with her partner, Gatlin, now sitting to her right, Lyndi and a team from the Gang Enforcement Unit had been working around the clock.

Flisk, sitting across the table, nodded at Lyndi. "Word is, the super's coming to this one," he said.

She looked up and nodded back. "You been home in a while?" she asked.

He shrugged.

"You look like shit," said Gatlin to Flisk.

"We all look like shit," he shot back.

"Not LC," said Gatlin, while giving her a once over.

"Yeah, well I get to cover it up with makeup," she said.

"You dump that public defender yet, the one that pissed himself in court awhile back?" asked Gatlin to Lyndi.

She only glared momentarily at him.

A large silver haired man entered the conference room, his police cap tucked under his right arm. He didn't wait for people to sit or lean against a wall. His voice boomed.

"The situation has escalated as you're all aware. Time is of the essence. I know there's been some rumblings about vigilantism on the street and the FBI, the DEA, or Homeland Security swooping in to take over the investigation," said Chicago Police Superintendent Michael O'Brien. "That's why we need to move quickly. Patrol is handling security in the troubled spots around the city. This group here is going to continue to handle the investigation. And for the time being it will remain headed up by Homicide, and Lead Detective Curtis.

"Let's go out there and show them what the Chicago Police Department can do before it gets passed off to either the FBI as serial in nature or possibly the DEA if there's evidence of a connection to the Sinaloa or Gulf cartels down in Mexico. Any information or evidence we find of those possibilities needs to be communicated through your chain of command accordingly and immediately.

"All yours, Fred."

Lyndi's boss, Fred Curtis, stood up and ran down all the evidence on the murders. At the end of his briefing, Curtis began doling out assignments to the officers in the room. When he got around to Lyndi and her partner, he seemed at a loss on where to send them or what to have them work on. Lyndi was irked. She and Gatlin had been the lead homicide investigators for the murders of The Scraper and Killer Joe, but now that this was turning into a full-fledged mass murder investigation, they were being pushed aside.

To break the awkward silence, she offered up an assignment. "Sir, we're following up on an earlier lead cultivated by Sergeant Flisk. See if we can glean more info from a source about an incident that took place in Back of the Yards, following the first murders."

"The hate crime?"

She was surprised he knew. "Yes, sir."

Detective Curtis shrugged and glanced over at another high-level officer standing across from him. It was the commander of the Gang Enforcement Unit, Flisk's boss. Curtis then looked back at Lyndi and nodded approval.

After the meeting Lyndi, Flisk and Gatlin gathered in a hallway. "What's up your boss's ass?" asked Gatlin to Flisk.

"He's a prick. He doesn't want me anywhere near this case."

"Why's that?" asked Lyndi.

Flisk tightened up his face. "Don't know, just doesn't like me."

"Well, he seems to think the hate crime on the street is a dead end, and that's why he's cutting you loose."

"Your boss seemed to think the same damn thing," said Flisk. "But why do you want to pursue that further?

Guy's an old man who lives in the hood. Some nut job went into the Yards one night probably high as hell and had a bad trip. Beat him up."

"But what about how you got involved, sergeant?" said Lyndi. "There was a connection with Raymond Delgado that night, too. He could be next in line. Or a suspect. Your initial follow up with Delgado didn't lead to anything?"

"Would only speak to us briefly, denied anything took place the night before. Listen, bangers don't cooperate with police even if it's a crime not related to them that we're investigating. It's not socially acceptable."

"I want to talk to this Mr. Hatch, get a description on the man and the car," said Lyndi. "You want to ride with us?"

Lyndi noticed that Flisk seemed to hesitate.

"Sure," he said finally.

CHAPTER FORTY

Harry remembered he was dying

HIS LEFT EYELID began twitching. Then, his left arm was shaking. His lungs froze up and his head flew back. He coughed out as much air as he could, while reaching for the pills on the nightstand. His outstretched arm tried desperately to reach the bottle, but when it did his body began convulsing and a shroud of blackness came over his eyes. Before losing consciousness, he could hear the pills rattle out of the bottle and his urine drip onto the floor.

If he had gotten to the pill bottle and was able to pop one or two into his mouth, he may have avoided waking up in his own piss with a raging headache. Doubled over, he shuffled his way back to bed, hacking and moaning. How long had it lasted? He didn't know. His tongue was sore, his mouth cotton dry.

The cellphone rang.

Unknown.

Harry grunted and tried to listen through the pain.

"I haven't heard from you in a while, my shepherd. The wolf needs to eat."

"Who is this?" asked Harry. He couldn't feel his mouth moving as he spoke. "What are you … talking about?"

"Name and location. Set something up for me soon or I'll case the streets for a young, fresh fowl to feast on. You hear men?"

"Who—"

"I never thought I'd get my fifteen minutes of fame, but I'm getting more than that now. I don't mind straying and finding me a sweet little innocent to sack. You want that on your conscience, my shepherd?"

"I don't know-I don't understand. I don't have any names."

"Name and location by tonight or I'm taking whomever I want—"

"I don't have any names! I don't know what you're—"

Harry felt relief when the call ended. He let his head fall heavily onto the mattress. He lay there, crumpled up in a fetal position, shivering.

And then a modicum of clarity kicked in, the seizure's aftershock had finally subsided.

Harry remembered he was dying.

CHAPTER FORTY-ONE

Men like that deserve a merciless death

FLISK TRIED TO move away from the window, but he found himself looking out it again. A glance every few seconds out front and then down the street. No one. The block empty of pedestrians, gangbangers.

He could hear Jebediah talking but he wasn't really listening.

"Frightened from the killings is what it is. Yards is a ghost town. Raymond Delgado thought of as immortal round here. Word is he aint been heard from nor seen in a while." Jebediah let out a short laugh. "They droppin like flies. No one wants to crawl out of their holes," continued the old man as Lyndi and Gatlin stood there listening. "You ask me, it's a blessin what's happening, a cleansing that shoulda been done a long time ago. Rid the streets of the cockroaches. But these rumors the news spews bout regular folk havin something to do with it? That's crazy. Yall got any ideas of who be doing it?" He held a toothpick firm in his mouth and slid his eyes to Gatlin.

Lyndi spoke up anyway. "That's why we're here. We're talking to everyone who has reported a violent crime in the area."

"So you think those bangers be victims, that it?" said Jebediah.

"Doesn't matter what I think, Mr. Hatch. It's my job to investigate homicides and turn any evidence I collect over to the DA's office. Do you have anyone who can verify the incident that took place in the street where Delgado was present?"

"I don't have many friends alive or 'round no mores," he said shyly, turning his head to look at Flisk, who caught the gesture and grinned. "I'm just an old man, like to watch PBS and sit on my porch listenin to the birds some evenings is all."

Flisk turned from the window and studied Jebediah's face.

Did the old man have enough balls to make Raymond Delgado disappear?

"It was a hot summer. I'm sure you were out there quite a bit," said Flisk to Jebediah.

"Not as hot as St. Louis gets in the summer time," replied Jebediah.

Lyndi noticed Flisk momentarily glare at the old man and thought it peculiar.

The exchange slipped her mind as she instructed Jebediah to take her through the night Delgado showed up when Jebediah was being assaulted by an individual out front of his home.

The more he explained the incident, the more questions Lyndi asked about the perpetrator. Jebediah gave every detail he could remember, right down to the specifics of the tattoos. When Gatlin asked if he'd had any other run-ins with the unknown perp or with Delgado since the initial incident, Jebediah hesitated to answer. His eyes shot up at Flisk, who quickly turned away.

"Nah, lucky for me they aint been 'round."

"Lucky for them, right Mr. Hatch?" said Flisk.

Jebediah grinned and nodded. "Yeah, I suppose, lucky for them. But," he turned and looked at Lyndi now, "the evil I saw in the eyes of both them men still haunts me. Knowing at least one of them is done breathing, well, that would be a relief. But I'd feel a whole lot better about everything if they was both dead." He looked down and seemed to stare at nothing, his mind preoccupied with thought. "Men like that deserve a merciless death."

"You have a weapon, Mr. Hatch?" asked Lyndi.

"I sure do. And I got a card, too."

"Mind if I take a look at it?"

Jebediah brought the weapon out of its holster in the small of his back, slid the magazine out and handed both to Lyndi.

"Impressive," she said. "You ever shoot it?"

"Not had to yet," he answered.

They both smiled. Lyndi knew instantly the old man had warmed to her.

"Mr. Hatch do you think you could identify your attacker?"

"I won't ever forget that man's face."

CHAPTER FORTY-TWO

Sorry, kid

LAQUAN POLK, DRESSED in his favorite Chicago Bulls T-shirt and athletic shorts, looked at the man suspiciously while bouncing a basketball on the cement court at a park near his godmother's house. He'd been shooting all morning with his cousin because they had heard it was supposed to rain later in the day. If that was the case, then they decided they'd just go over to another cousin's house who had Xbox and play NBA 2K14.

"You got James' autograph on a rock and you givin it away?" he asked again.

When the man nodded, LaQuan began to walk toward him, still dribbling the ball.

LaQuan's cousin called out, "Q, don't go with him. He aint got no such thing. He's playin ya."

Stopping and looking back, LaQuan replied defiantly, "It's King James, baby!"

"He gonna rob you, you got any dough on you," said his cousin.

But LaQuan continued to follow the man, mumbling back at his cousin, "He gonna rob a nine-year-old with nothin but a basketball?"

He could hear his cousin's voice trail off as he walked away, "I just wouldn't go if I was you!"

LaQuan followed the man out of the park and across the street. They went two blocks before he looked up and asked, "Where you have the ball at?"

"My garage."

"You got an autographed King James ball sittin in your garage? Man, that's disrespectful."

"That's right. C'mon, quit askin questions."

Excited about the prospect of having a free autographed LeBron James basketball, LaQuan followed the man into an alley, dribbling, crossing over, slipping the ball behind his back, through his legs, head faking and drop-stepping. When the man turned around and asked him a question he didn't hear him, too busy pretending to be an NBA star.

"I said yer daddy is Lucifer Polk, aint it?"

LaQuan stopped dribbling suddenly and looked up. "My daddy?"

"Yer LaQuan Polk, aint you?"

"I don't know my daddy."

The man reached his right hand behind his back. "But your momma is a Polk, aint she?"

"My last name is Polk. Momma's name is Keisha. She works at a baby nursery. I'm gonna be King Q on the court someday, build us a mansion with a pool! So, which garage you got the rock in?"

"*Lo siento, niño.* Sorry, kid."

*****

Blocks away in the park, sitting on a bench, LaQuan's cousin heard five gunshots. He knew right away they were gunshots. He had heard the sound many times before.

He wasn't the first to find his cousin. A large group had gathered around the body. LaQuan's godmother was on her knees wailing and yelling something awful at Jesus.

He made his way to the body as the roar of sirens grew nearer. He looked at LaQuan and all the blood that soaked his Chicago Bulls T-shirt, and then picked up his cousin's basketball.

He walked away down the alley, back toward the park, dribbling the ball.

CHAPTER FORTY-THREE

Don't shoot me!

ON ONE SIDE of Rockwell an enormous empty lot, fenced all around, weeds growing between the cracks of the cement, stretched on for two city blocks. Buildings had been razed not so long ago. On the other side of Rockwell a brick warehouse took up an entire block, a dark entrance to a loading dock in its center.

It was an overcast day, had been drizzling for much of the morning.

Quiet and peaceful, thought the officer, not like the damn corners in the Austin neighborhood.

"But these car owners are gonna be pissed come quittin time," he said to himself as he finished writing another ticket for parking too long in a two-hour spot. He ripped the ticket from his book and shoved it under a windshield wiper, then began to walk to the next car.

A squad car pulled up and stopped. "Hey kid, how many you got left?"

The officer turned and looked down the street. He saw the end where an overpass stretched across the road. "Only a few," he replied.

"Alright, Kowalski. I could eat a god damn horse's ass twice on Sunday. Finish up, we're going to Mannies. I'm gonna get some gas around the block and swing back and pick your newbie ass up."

Kowalski nodded. When the squad car rolled away, he said aloud, "Newbie? That's fresh, Murphy. What a fat fuck," and began writing out another ticket.

It wasn't long after when Kowalski noticed that one of the parked cars fit the description of a vehicle that had been carjacked earlier in the day. It was a black Honda Accord. Kowalski was sure the plates matched the bulletin. He was about to notify his supervisor when he noticed movement in the front seat.

"Oh shit."

Two men popped up out of the car and immediately spotted the officer. Kowalski drew his weapon and told them to freeze, but they took off. He followed one toward the empty lot. As the man jumped on the fence to climb over it, Kowalski grabbed him by his belt and flung him to the ground. He held him down with a knee and looked up for the other man.

"Leave that boy alone, copper!" someone yelled from across the street. "He's done nothin wrong."

"Don't shoot me!" pleaded the young man on the ground.

Kowalski was about to put away his gun and call for backup when he spotted the second man from the car gaiting towards him. He raised the weapon.

"Stop where you are!"

"Get off my brother! He just scared is all. You spooked us."

Kowalski told the man again to stop where he was or he would shoot. The man put up his arms but kept coming.

"You stop there and we will sort this out!" Kowalski tried to shout over the man. "Why aren't you listening?"

The impact shoved Kowalski upward before his legs went out from under him. Everything went dark and he hit the sidewalk hard on his back. When he opened his eyes, he reached for his gun but it wasn't there. He raised himself up by his hands but his legs wouldn't move, wouldn't bend. A sharp pain ripped down his spine, and he fell back down onto his back again.

Seeing his gun in the street a few feet away, he managed to turn over onto his belly and crawl for it. He sensed he was crawling through a puddle, but looking under him he saw that his blue uniform was now dark red. He stopped and rolled onto his back again. He was now looking up at the young man he had pulled off the fence."

"I wasn't going to shoot anyone," Kowalski pleaded.

A bullet hit him in the center of his forehead and his body went limp.

CHAPTER FORTY-FOUR

Shot and killed

News Report

Chicago burning: Nine-year-old murdered, cop killed in cold blood

Governor considering calling up National Guard to restore order

WITHIN A SPAN of just four hours yesterday, a nine-year-old boy was lured into an alley and shot and killed because of his father's association with a rival gang, and a rookie police officer was shot and killed on the street in what investigators are calling a hate crime spurred by the ongoing racial tensions now citywide, according to police officials.

Police say LaQuan Polk, of the 800 block of Carlisle Avenue, was playing basketball with a relative in Garfield Park near his godmother's home when he was lured into an alley and shot multiple times. He died at the scene.

Police officials say that the killing is likely in connection to Polk's father being affiliated with a local gang. Lucifer Polk, 32, no known address available, a notorious gang member who has been in and out of jail several times in the last decade has not been seen or heard from in weeks.

Later in the day and less than a mile away, on the near west side, officer Bryan Kowalski was gunned down in the street while issuing parking tickets on Washington Blvd.

Craig Maloney, 27, who works at Ideal Metal Fabricators on the block, said he was leaving at the end of his shift when he witnessed the officer trying to apprehend a young man before being shot at point-blank range.

"I don't know if maybe the guy was just enraged and went berserk, upset that he had gotten a ticket or something."

Kowalski was shot multiple times and died at the scene. Police say they have no suspects at this time but are following up on several leads.

Illinois Governor Tim Buchanan held a hastily thrown together press conference yesterday evening in front of the Dirksen Courthouse where he said he was not ruling out calling up the National Guard to restore order in Chicago.

"As many in the city and in the nation are aware, Chicago is currently mired in more than just a gang crisis. Due to the escalation of gang violence and racial tensions there is a dire need for a more robust response," said the governor. "And right now we are working on outlining that response in order to curtail the bloodshed and restore order to this city.

Buchanan first discussed a potential role for the National Guard earlier in the summer during a television interview after Jaylen Roy was gunned down while holding a pocket knife in the street by a Chicago police officer in Englewood. Since then, a family was found slain in a home in Gage Park which authorities have alluded may be related to a Mexican cartel dispute. Ten gang leaders have also been murdered in the span of nearly three months, but authorities have yet to announce possible motives.

Police Superintendent Michael O'Brien would only say that a team of investigators is currently following up on leads to see whether or not the murders fall outside the realm of the city's notorious gangland warfare.

"We're basically working several massive investigations here," he said. "Our priority is to find the perpetrators for each homicide and bring them to justice and to determine if this goes beyond gang retribution."

When asked to elaborate, O'Brien alluded to the possibility that the gang leader murders could be related to a feud between large Mexican cartels or "serial in nature by an individual or a faction."

"We're looking at everything, and we're getting help on the federal level," he said before the press conference was abruptly concluded.

CHAPTER FORTY-FIVE

We have enough blood on our hands

A COMMAND CENTER had been set up in a large conference room of the Chicago Police Department's main building. Lyndi sat at a desk, pouring over the crime scene photos. The blood smears at some of the crime scenes were perplexing. She grabbed a piece of paper and drew out each marking. On paper they were simply an assortment of horizontal and vertical lines, but she felt there had to be a connection to something.

Just then her cellphone buzzed. It was her boss, Detective Curtis, he wanted to see her right away in his office.

When she arrived another man she recognized but did not know personally was leaning against a file cabinet. It was the commander of the Gang Enforcement Unit. Curtis made the brief introductions.

"Lyndi, this is Commander Wayne Martinson, Gang Enforcement. Wayne, Homicide Detective Lyndi Carnes."

Lyndi and Curtis sat, while Martinson kept his position standing and leaning on the file cabinet. He was a heavyset man with gray hair, a thick mustache and several moles that pocked the dark skin of his face.

"Detective, how's it going?" asked Curtis.

"Well, under the circumstances, sir, it's just going," answered Lyndi. "We're doing what we can."

"I've never taken so much Pepto-Bismol in my life," joked Curtis, but Martinson didn't even smirk.

"Lyndi, you've been working closely with Sergeant Flisk, is that correct?" asked Martinson.

She nodded.

"Well, how has he been conducting himself during the investigation?"

Lyndi looked from Martinson to Curtis. "What is this?"

Curtis frowned. "Wayne, Detective Carnes is not one to—"

"Fuck with," finished Lyndi.

"Right," said Curtis, a blush emanating from his face. "Just get to the punch, please."

Martinson came away from the file cabinet. "Fine. Has Sergeant Flisk shown any sign of reluctance to carry out his duties during this investigation?"

"Again, what is this—"

"Detective, we want you to keep an eye on Sergeant Flisk. Report anything he may do or say that you deem out of the ordinary or suspicious."

"You're worried about a possible dirty cop with all the shit that's going on out there?"

"We don't know. But they could be related," said Martinson.

"Wait a minute, Wayne," Curtis interjected, "We're not speculating. You asked if Detective Carnes could keep her eyes and ears open for anything strange, that's it. Let's not give this guy a bad rap and start any rumors here. We have enough on our hands."

"We have enough blood on our hands," added Lyndi, staring down Martinson. "Internal accusations like that at a time like this could only fuel unrest. Tell me, please, that you think he's just shaking down a petty dealer for walking around cash."

"I'm not at liberty to say, but he's got a checkered past. Ten dead minorities, even if they can be described as the scum of the earth, killed as if someone had inside information, is quite a peculiar set of circumstances when you know what I know."

Lyndi shook her head exasperated. "Unless this is cartel related, there doesn't seem to be a motive other than the thrill of killing these scumbags. If you're gonna base your judgement on that, put me on your suspect list as well. Hell, put half of Chicago on your fuckin list."

Martinson sat on the end of the desk, in front of Lyndi. "Detective, isn't there enough animosity out there on the streets right now? The city's an inferno and the department is dealing with one of its biggest public calamities in its history.

"Chicago has become the mecca of violent crimes and widespread corruption. Every cop is being scrutinized for his or her actions."

"Are you not concerned about the welfare of your fellow officers, commander?" snapped Lyndi.

"Easy now, you two. Cut the crap," said Curtis. "We don't know what is playing out here, for god's sake."

Martinson kept his eyes on Lyndi. He cleared his throat and spoke at a more even tone. "Sergeant Flisk has a history of being involved in high-profile cases, and we want to make sure this is not a coincidence."

"Thanks for clarifying," said Lyndi as she got up from her chair. "Can I get back to my job, now?"

*****

The first thing Lyndi did when she arrived back at her desk was open up her laptop and search Flisk's name on the internet. She found nothing of interest. But when she recalled the look Flisk and Mr. Hatch gave one another when St. Louis came up during their talk about the hate crime, she searched other, more general terms. After a while, a few headlines caught her eye. She read the stories and clicked on the images to see a man who looked similar to Flisk, though he was slimmer and had no beard.

Unarmed black 12-year-old boy shot and killed by white Fenton police officer

Four men and a 12-year-old boy were killed in a shooting that involved a Fenton police officer in the alley near Bloomfield and Galewood on Tuesday afternoon.

According to Tom Kline, spokesperson for the Fenton Police Department, the shooting occurred after an officer stopped a car for rolling through a stop sign near the intersection of Bloomfield near Ron Hayes Elementary School.

"This is an ongoing investigation and because it's a police officer involved shooting, it's being handed over to the Missouri State Police," he said.

Kline said details of the shooting were still being gathered but initial reports indicate that officer Dale Fisher was confronted by a group of men, who may or may not have been armed. A verbal altercation ensued before shots were fired, according to witnesses.

"The cop just shot up everybody. They weren't doing nothing but sitting minding they own business in the garage, trying to stay cool in this awful heat is all," said Tonia Madsen, a homeowner near the scene. "His police car pulled in behind that Cadillac and he got out and the young fella just asked what it was all about and then it was the fourth of July all over again. Kids were killed. Children. A baby!"

Madsen said she witnessed the incident from a kitchen window a few houses down from the shooting.

Kline added that a weapon was located at the scene as well as on a person of interest who was apprehended a few blocks away.

"Officials still need to be briefed by the officer involved and responding officers," said Kline. "The department is in the process of interviewing witnesses."

The deceased have yet to be identified pending notification of next of kin.

Former Fenton police officer cleared of rights violations in shooting

Six months after a grand jury decided not to indict former Fenton Police officer Dale Fisher for the killing of an unarmed 12-year-old boy during a shootout that stirred racially charged protests across the country, the U.S. Department of Justice has cleared the officer of civil rights violations.

In a forty page report that detailed and evaluated the testimony of more than twenty-five witnesses, the Justice Department largely corroborated or found little credible evidence to contradict the account of the officer for the killing of Marcus Jackson, a seventh grader.

The report stated the versions of events that conflicted with Fisher's were largely inconsistent with forensic evidence.

Fisher pulled over a car in August for not stopping at a stop sign. According to the initial report, the offenders immediately became hostile and would not cooperate with the officer, who called for backup. Before additional officers arrived, a shootout occurred.

Several weapons were found at the scene that were traced back to being fired by William Foldham, 28, Charles Platt, 24, and Ronald Gray, 24, all killed at the scene by Fisher's service weapon. It was determined that Jackson, the 12-year-old killed at the scene, was hit by crossfire, also from Fisher's service weapon.

Wayne Tinley, 23, was apprehended two blocks away with an Uzi that had been used to kill Lyle Coldwell, 38, who had come upon the scene while turning into the alley on his way home from work.

Images of Jackson lying dead at the scene and initial witness accounts that turned out to be false, spread across media platforms within hours, causing violent riots across the country that lasted months.

After receiving multiple death threats, Fisher resigned from the department shortly after the incident. Attempts at reaching Fisher for a comment for this story were unsuccessful.

*****

Lyndi looked up from the computer screen to find both Flisk and Gatlin standing in front of her.

"Hello? This is the second and last time I'm asking: Do you want to go grab a cold one with us?" said Flisk.

CHAPTER FORTY-SIX

I have what I need

RAYMOND DELGADO REMINDED himself that it was simply a matter of tying up loose ends. It had to be done.

He parked the SUV by the garage and unloaded four five-gallon containers of gasoline. He had filled up each one at four different gas stations as to not look suspicious.

It was perfect. Tiny had been the one who had met with the owner of the home and set up the rent payments. Nobody knew Raymond Angel Delgado out in Hinsdale. Tiny's Jeep was parked in the driveway. As far as anyone was concerned, Tiny was renting and living at this mini-mansion himself.

The garage door went up and there was the big man sitting on a step that led into the house, a dower look on his face.

"I think he knew, boss," he said.

"You think he knew what, Tiny?"

"You know, that he wasn't leaving here."

"Help me with the gas cans. Take them inside."

"What do you want with the gas cans, boss?"

"Take two of them upstairs and splash them around the place. Bring the other two downstairs."

"You're going to burn this beautiful house down, boss?"

Delgado ignored him and went straight down to the basement. Several bundled up stacks of cash sat in the open on a table, two bill counting machines next to them. On another table were two large piles of cash, the bills yet to be counted and bundled.

On the floor, wrapped in clear plastic, was the body of Edgar Rojas. Delgado stepped over his former friend and began loading the stacks of cash into a duffel bag. When he was finished he scooped up a couple of hand-fuls of the cash from the pile on the other table and stuffed them into the bag. But then he stopped himself. A thought crossed his mind.

Just then, Tiny came down the stairs lugging two of the gas containers.

"I did what you said to do, boss. Gas, it stinking up the place up there."

"Tiny, what did you use to kill Rojas?"

Tiny put down the gas containers and pointed to a corner of the basement where a three-foot long iron pipe leaned against the wall. Delgado went over and picked it up, studying it and weighing it in his hands.

He looked over at Tiny. "Okay, start dousing the basement and I'll meet you upstairs."

"What about this cash, boss? You gonna just let it burn? There are thousands of dollars in that pile."

Delgado knew the stupid lug would bite. "I have what I need. You want it, go ahead," he said.

Tiny's eyes lit up. "Sure, boss. *Gracias.*" He grabbed a duffel bag and bent down just as Delgado figured the moron would.

Raising it well above him and using all the weight and leverage he could muster, Delgado smashed the iron pipe down onto Tiny's head. The blunt sound and the blood splatter spooked Delgado for a moment. He quickly wiped blood from his face and focused on his victim, who hadn't fallen next to Rojas, but was stumbling about, bent over and holding his head, moaning.

Delgado took two steps and swung the iron pipe again, this time landing it directly on Tiny's right temple. The big man punctured a hole in the drywall with his weight and slid down to the floor. Dull-eyed, he sat there looking up at his boss, blood streaming down his shattered face.

"You ratted Rojas out to Los Zetas, Tiny. And this is what becomes of rats. They are left to die in basements."

Delgado picked up one of the gas containers and emptied it onto Tiny, who was fading in and out of consciousness. He picked up the other one and spread the gas all over the basement walls.

After finding a utility lighter, Delgado gathered up the duffel bag full of money and lit the pile of cash on the table. He went up the stairs and into the kitchen where he opened the oven door, turned on the gas and ignited all the gas burners.

"*Adios*, America," he said as he went out the door and hopped into the SUV. But before pulling out of the long, winding driveway, he sat there looking at the house.

It is a beautiful home. Alexa was a beautiful woman, and eventually would have made a fine wife and mother.

He thought about the unborn child now, pictured the little man running around the large driveway, kicking a ball. The sorrow washed over him again, and he looked at the duffel bag full of money sitting next to him in the passenger's seat.

"*Jesús salva.* Jesus saves," he said.

CHAPTER FORTY-SEVEN

You're not long on this earth

LABORIOUSLY, HARRY LIFTED himself out of his car. He shuffled over and leaned on the hood. He was out of breath and fluttering his eyelids, trying to clear his sight. He hadn't eaten anything solid in days. Thin and weak, he could barely stand.

The abandoned railyard was quiet, just lines of rust colored tracks, a few weathered and graffiti-ridden rail-cars and an old warehouse building off in the distance.

A cloud of dust came twisting up the road. A beat-up gray Camaro. It stopped at Harry's car. A ripped and tatted up man got out.

"Why did you want to meet?" coughed Harry.

"Because I need more names, friend. I need a fix! I'm jonesing!" He let out a sinister laugh. "I'm like a su-perhero to these people and I need to feed them more and more and feed myself more and more. Now give me a fuckin name and a location so I can give the public want it wants."

"I am not your friend and I don't have to do anything you tell me to do." Harry bent over, his hands on his knees.

"You think I care about your pathetic life? I'll rat you out and they'll send you up to Leavenworth where you'll be some convict's bitch."

He only looked up at Leroy Crump pathetically. "Are you really that stupid?"

"Watch what you say to me, or I'll get off on you, friend. I'll give the people a lawyer neggar to mourn."

It took everything he had to throw the punch, but Harry had nothing to lose. His fist landed square on the right side of Crump's jaw, but the man barely flinched. Crump shoved Harry to the ground.

"I do respect your tenacity, but I'm growing quite bored."

"What do you need me for?" asked Harry, his voice dry and desperate as he sat in the dirt, leaning exhaustively on the car. "Just go do whatever you want without me."

"I've explained it to you. You're my shepherd and you're to bring the big bad wolf the sheep to slaughter. We're in it together."

"You're a sociopath and a danger to society. You're nothing but evil. You're the exact definition of evil. You're an evil, psycho sunuvabitch, Leroy Crump!"

Crump let out a loud, wet laugh. "Evil? That's precious coming from you!"

"No more," croaked Harry. "It's over."

"Nothin is ever over, my shepherd. Spend some time in prison and you'll find out time has no end."

"Life has an end."

"You talkin about death? Life is a continuation of death and vice versa. There's no beginning and no end. Now, give me a name and location. I'm jonesing. It's like if I don't get it I'll explode, self-combust."

"You're mentally ill. You know that, right?"

"There you go again. Sick in the head? Look who's talking. Why can't you just admit to it? I know you've felt it. I could see it in your face after you found out about the first two we put down. You were more than willing to get the names to us.

"You see, my shepherd, you're no different than me. You're a stone-cold killer yourself."

"You get off on it. I was doing it for—"

"Every man has his desires. Yours happens to be a female homicide detective with firm tits and a tight little ass. Be a shame anything ever happened to her."

"Anything happens to her and—"

"And what, my shepherd? Look at you, you're not long on this earth. I may just be a good friend and bring her to you some day." Crump squatted down next to Harry. "Would you like that? Would you like to see that ass in purgatory?"

"One more," Harry said, his voice defiantly stronger. "The last one. I'll get you another shot at Raymond Delgado. Just don't go blowing it again this time. Tomorrow, noon, far west of the city. Take the Eisenhower out, it will turn into Interstate Eighty-Eight. Past the burbs. You'll see nothing but a long stretch of fields. Take the Peace Road exit south. Down aways you'll see an abandoned farmhouse. Well behind it and a thick grove of trees is a pond. They'll be expecting you— they'll be expecting me."

"It sounds like you're trying to ambush me, my shepherd."

"Stop calling me that, you fuckin wack-job!"

Crump slapped Harry across the face and Harry fell onto his side near the front tire of the car.

"Why so far out of the city? No banger ventures too far from his crib."

Harry slowly raised himself back to a sitting position, blood trickling from his lip. "It's getting more and more difficult drawing them out," he said in-between catching his breath. "I have to go through channels now. They don't want to meet in public. Too risky." He spit blood onto the dirt. "Just trust me! But this is it. No more after this one."

"It may be the last one for you, my shepherd, but it certainly won't be the last for me. The wolf must be fed."

CHAPTER FORTY-EIGHT

We all have a past

GATLIN HAD JUST stammered out of the bar with a woman on his arm, looking back at both Lyndi and Flisk and waving, "If our lil meeting is over, I'm leaving. See you tomorrow … or not."

Lyndi took a sip of her beer and looked back up at the television. She silently scolded herself for wondering if Harry had been watching the Cubs in the National League Championship Series.

"Jimmy, double shot of Makers, please," she said to the barkeep as most of the patrons took to the exits following the game.

She noticed Flisk wipe his face with his hand as if he were wiping away frustration. When he picked up his mug of beer and drank most of it down, she grew annoyed and felt compelled to ask him what his problem was, but thought better of it. Instead, she went into why the three of them had convened at the bar in the first place: to discuss Jebediah Hatch's perpetrator and whether or not there was a possible connection to the murders of the gang leaders. She figured by morning they'd get the call to back off the gang murders and put all their resources to use on the cop slaying.

"Did you get anything off the neighbors?"

She caught the hint of bewilderment in Flisk's face.

"The hate crime in Back of the Yards. You were going to ask around the neighborhood, and your CIs, see if anyone witnessed the assault and Delgado's presence at it."

"Yeah, no. Not even a 'hello officer, we're sorry to hear about what happened to one of your fellow officers,' came my way. Just the finger and a 'fuck off.'"

"They're riled from all the killing, which doesn't sit well no matter who the dead are," said Lyndi. "The cop was a rook, didn't see it coming. A little experience on the force goes a long way." She downed her shot and ordered another beer. "One for the coroner, Jimmy," she said with a smile.

She felt Flisk looking at her. "That's cold, you know? What about the kid shot in the face because his father was a gangbanger? His fault, too? You know, detective, you may be something to look at and a hell of ball breaker, but you have a cold, sick way of looking at things."

"You sound like most of my ex-guy friends."

When she turned and faced him again, she watched the anger subside from his eyes and brow. She'd seen it before in men, that scowl thaw to nothing. But never from Harry West. Harry never became angry at how heartless she could be. He just let her be who she was.

Sure, he was bewildered by it, but never angry. Maybe he kept it to himself. Damn, there was Harry again.

Flisk broke her thought with, "You want to ask me about something, detective?"

Well, now's a good time, she thought. "What's your history, sergeant?"

He didn't even pause. "Rosemary, my sister, was six years old when some guy tried to lure her into his car in front of the house.

"It was from that incident that I wanted to become a police officer." He put his head back as if he were recalling the scene in his mind. "A neighbor had seen it unfold and called the Jennings Police Department. They descended with sirens blaring, lights flashing, and I stood awed by the controlled chaos. I was mesmerized by their uniforms, their toughness, their sympathy, their teamwork, their ability to quickly locate the offender and apprehend him. For a snot-nosed kid like me it was like watching real superheroes at work.

"The Jennings Police Department was on a hiring freeze for a while, but I got a break when a spot opened up in Fenton, just up West Florissant Avenue."

"You're from Missouri?" asked Lyndi, trying not to reveal what she knew.

He snorted a laugh before adding, "It's funny how fate works. I had no idea back then that in a few years' time the whole country would know my name and that eventually I would have to pick up my family and move away." He finished his beer and ordered another, plus a shot of tequila.

Lyndi shook her head. "Shit just kind of follows you, Flisk. And, man, did you sure as hell pick the wrong city to relocate to."

The way he looked at Lyndi she could tell he appreciated the humor and the fact that she addressed him personally. Not to mention she had not shown any shock or surprise by his revelation.

He let out a quick laugh again. "Figured you wouldn't react too much to my past." He rubbed his chin, and then his face turned serious. "Well, no one can predict the future. How was I to know that a white cop was going to shoot a black teenager sixteen times in the middle of the street and somebody would start killing off gang leaders, and nut-jobs would gun down a cop, and kids and families would be killed—yeah I walked right out of one mess, into another."

"We all have a past," she said absentmindedly and turned and swigged her beer, thoughts of both her father and Harry meshing in her mind.

Harry is a good man, she told herself. He wasn't her father. No man could ever live up to that image. She needed to tell Harry that it was fear that made her so tough, that caused her to put up walls. Fear of someone she cared so much about leaving her for good. Harry wouldn't leave ... but he did. And now it was hitting her. Harry had left. No man had ever left, except for her father.

"So, detective, you mentioned your ex-guy friends. What's that mean, boyfriends? Are you on hiatus or something? I mean what is it you do with your spare time? Any friends or family?"

He was on the cusp of flirting. She could see it in his blue-green eyes, probably too alarmed at his own vulnerability.

"I had—have a friend. A public defender. His name's Harry West."

"Oh, yeah. I know him. The lawyer too good at his job who passed out during a sentencing hearing."

"Well, everyone has bad days, right?" she padded Flisk on the shoulder. She could sense they had connected and that the same registered for him. She threw down a twenty and grabbed her coat off the barstool.

"I'll drink to that," she heard Flisk say as she started for the door.

"Go home to your wife and kid, Flisk. We've got work to do tomorrow."

CHAPTER FORTY-NINE

Pleading wouldn't do any good

HE FOUND ME not long after he got out of prison. I had backed my car into the garage and when I stopped and looked forward there he was, the devil himself, a menacing silhouette at dusk back-dropped by an urban alleyway. Horns and all.

He had added a ridiculous amount of tattoos to the skin that wasn't covered up. A spider web was inked across his bald head.

Looking at his menacing eyes, I could tell he wasn't there for a cordial visit. I got out and tried to make a run for it. A spade caught me on the back of the head and the pain seared in my skull. It wasn't as bad as the vicious pain of the frequent migraines I'd been experiencing for some time, but I was on my knees tasting blood, a thick tatted up arm wrapped firmly around my neck. I was being choked out, looking up at a portly young woman with a baby's face. She was kicking me in the nuts but missing and hitting upper-thigh-upper-thigh-upper-thigh.

As I choked, coughed and spat blood from my lips, he dragged me into my own house by the collar, dumped me on the kitchen floor, drove a knee into my rib cage and then made the portly woman sit on me.

The knife looked like one of mine from the block on the counter. He stuck it stiff, but delicately—a flesh wound—in my left armpit and said, "Hello, counselor, it's your favorite former client. Come to pay my respects for a job well done."

From the moment I saw the silhouette in the doorway of my garage I knew that it was Leroy Crump. You don't forget your first client, not when he's a violent racist and you're of mixed race trying to keep him out of prison for the rest of his life.

Pleading wouldn't do any good. Reasoning was out of the question. Even though I recalled negotiating a plea deal that this lunatic obviously approved, it seems, after being locked up awhile, he had changed his feelings about it. And I was to pay. Tortured first, likely. Maybe raped—despite my efforts, Leroy was in prison a long god-damn time. Maybe he'd burn me alive. Chop me up. Throw a noose around my neck and hang me from the maple tree out front. Leave a cross burning in my yard as I lay dead inside. The guy was a nut job.

There I was waiting for the end, wondering if I'd done enough in my life. What did I see, hear, smell and touch for the last time? What did I do? Did I make enough of a difference with my time? Why hadn't I married yet? Why wasn't I a father?

He squatted down next to my face on the floor, his breath metal. "You and me are going on a mission, counselor," he had said, cords of veins ripping from his tattooed neck.

"Where are we going?" I struggled to spit from my mouth, my ribs bruised and burning from the weight of this woman.

"It's not a physical journey, counselor. It's a spiritual ride. You see, I been apprised of a revelation that the almighty Adam, man of Genesis, has passed unto me. The day of reckoning has come. And you're going to be the shepherd that brings me the sheep."

"What the hell are you talking about?"

"Ah now, wait for the best part: I'm going to be the big bad wolf doing the slaughtering."

He slashed the knife across my right leg, tearing through my pants and skin but not too deeply, not muscle, just enough for me to writhe in pain and feel the warm blood trickle down to my ankle.

"Fat Annie and my Aryan Nation brethren are gonna eradicate the scum from this earth. One-by-one. You, my shepherd, are going to help corral them for us."

A skinhead who wants my help in eradicating ... I said what the fuck?

If I didn't go through with it, he said he'd skin me alive. When I said no you're going back to prison, shit-for-brains, the woman got off me and he drove his knee down into my sternum, then said, "You're damn honorable. Look at you. It's been your life's work keeping them out of the pen and now you're willing to give your life up for them.

"Well, I thought it may come to this. I know about your lil detective girlfriend. You may be alright with sacrificing YOUR LIFE, but are you alright with sacrificing her life?"

"Why don't you just start your cleansing with me, asshole?" I said. "Do I need to remind you again that I'm black?"

"Kill the shepherd?" He feigned surprise. "Well, that would hinder the mission. And besides we aint just doing it out of duty, we get pure pleasure from it. Aint that right, Fat Annie?" He turned his attention toward the woman and smacked her backside as she grinned. He gave me a deadline and strolled out the backdoor holding the woman by a fistful of her hair in one hand and the knife in the other.

Later, after getting a few stiches in my noggin and receiving the results from a CT scan of my head injury from the spade—I had told the ER docs I had fallen down some stairs—I found out the reason for the migraines and the blurred vision that I had been experiencing for months.

I was told to see a specialist, who ran more tests and promptly informed me I was diagnosed with terminal brain cancer.

It was right in the middle of the Delgado trial, so I didn't have time to think much about it. Maybe I didn't want to anyway.

-HJW

CHAPTER FIFTY

Say hello to the devil for me

HARRY KEPT IT in the firebox. It was buried under insurance forms, car and home titles, receipts and other documents. Pulling it out, he was surprised he had kept it all these years.

A simple .22 caliber snub-nose single-action revolver, black steel but a worn out faded handle. A rudimentary wheel gun back in the day.

Harry studied it oddly. It appeared so diminutive and antiquated compared to the handguns on television and in movies, compared to the handguns of police officers and those he'd seen as evidence when working cases. But loaded, pointed at close range directly at someone's head, it would get the job done.

How strange, he thought, as he recalled purchasing the gun for protection after defending his first client,

Leroy Crump. And now he was retrieving it from the firebox because of the same man.

Can I do this?

He quickly dismissed the question. He had the balls. He was a dying man. A dying man has the biggest balls. A dying man can do whatever the hell he wants to do.

He shoved the gun into his back jean pocket and had to quickly re-adjust his belt at the waist. Harry frowned when there wasn't a notch left on the belt to cinch his pants. He had lost so much weight in such a short time. He was withering away. No appetite. No taste buds. No sense of smell. The nauseous feeling was the only feeling. It had gotten so bad that he was either vomiting or on the verge of vomiting.

He stammered around the house hunched over, fumbling for items that he needed for the day. He found a dark coat and a pair of shoes, snagged the legal pad and a pen off the kitchen counter and stumbled to the couch where he plopped down exhausted.

After a few minutes of catching his breath, Harry leafed through the legal pad to a blank page and began to write Lyndi a final note in case he didn't make it back. When he was finished he set the legal pad on the coffee table and took a deep breath. It was time to go.

The nausea and the blurred vision made the sixty-mile drive difficult on Harry, but it was nothing compared to the throbbing headache that emerged as he veered off the interstate and took the Peace Road exit ramp. As he approached the driveway to the abandoned farmhouse, he saw no cars anywhere on the property. He slowed and pulled to the side of the road. Harry popped open a prescription bottle and downed a couple of pain-killers. He took a gulp of water and then sat back and tried desperately not to vomit it up.

Just then he caught a glimpse of his reflection in the rearview mirror. His face was gaunt and his skin pale except for gray streaks under his eyes. He had a layer of sweat on his face and his forehead held beads of it. Harry shook his head at the reflection as tears welled up in his eyes.

How did I end up like this? It all went so fast. In the blink of an eye.

It was a brisk autumn morning and the cold air felt refreshing on Harry's burning temples. He held his stomach and stammered hunched over as he made his way along the crick to the cluster of trees, stopping along the way to catch his breath. As he neared the tree line, he looked up: a colossal of bright and beautiful yellow, orange, and red colors. Harry straightened and took it in. He watched as a high breeze gently brushed the leaves and they came floating downward, over him and resting at his feet.

He wiped more tears from his eyes and then stumbled past the tree line. Finding a wide enough trunk near the pond to prop himself up, Harry pulled out the .22. He let his back slide down the tree until he was sitting, breathing hard, blinking away the blurriness.

A long fifteen minutes later, he could here footsteps approaching, shoes kicking up the leaves, the sound moving down the slope toward the pond. Harry struggled to raise himself up. He cocked the hammer back on the gun and stepped out from behind the tree. He raised the gun with both hands and pointed it at Crump.

But it wasn't him. It was a short, disheveled looking man in a jean jacket with no sleeves. A cigarette dangling from his lips. The man raised up his tatted arms and took a drag from the cigarette, blowing the smoke out his nostrils.

Harry felt a taut grip at the back of his neck and watched the gun disappear from his hands. He recognized Leroy Crump's voice.

"You're in no shape to be playin with guns," Crump said as he dragged Harry from the collar down to a landing near the pond and deposited him there like he was a sack of potatoes.

The pain in Harry's knees was nothing compared to the throbbing in his head. He knelt there crumpled over, trying to catch his breath, hoping another seizure wasn't forthcoming.

Crump squatted, leaned into Harry's ear and whispered.

Harry sat there in a daze. He was powerless. No weapon. No energy to even lift himself from the leaf-draped ground. He slumped further down onto his back.

He tried not to keep what Crump had whispered in his fractured brain for too long. But it flashed again.

"Let the wolf put you out of your poor misery, shepherd." A sinister laugh, and, "Say hello to the devil for me."

Harry willed the words from his mind by trying to imagine something beautiful and complete. This was the exact spot he had held Lyndi in his arms just a few months before. He thought about her now, her skin, her hair draped on her shoulder, her smile. He only saw her in his arms and not Crump standing over him, pointing a pistol down at his chest and firing two slugs.

His body writhed. He held the image in his head for as long as possible.

Looking up at the crown of the trees, the glorious autumn colors, leaves whisking from the top and falling gently down around him, Harry grinned.

The second Harry's eyes froze into a blank stare, Crump's mouth fell open and he let out a long euphoric sigh. "Hey, dog! Get down here and get a whiff of this!"

Fat Annie stumbled down the slope holding a semiautomatic rifle.

Crump, Annie and the man in the sleeveless jean jacket sat down near the pond. They passed around a small pipe stuffed with marijuana.

"Yes sir. This is a good day for the wolf," said Crump. He turned and put his arm around Annie. "A real good day for the wolf and his dog."

"What's next, Leroy?" asked the man in the sleeveless jean jacket, giggling.

Crump toked the pipe and took a hit, holding the smoke in his lungs. He exhaled slowly through his mouth and said, "Well, a celebration is in order. We go home and have a party. Mission accomplished."

Annie and the man in the sleeveless jean jacket smiled and nodded approval. They passed the pipe back to Crump, who took another hit. "And then we might as well kill us a neggar-lovin cop."

CHAPTER FIFTY-ONE

I'm going dark on this

FROM THE OUTSIDE, the bungalow looked dark and quiet. She peered into the foyer through a slit of glass and rapped again on the door. There was no movement from inside. She tried calling him on her cellphone from right there at the front door but his phone went to voicemail.

She wanted to see him, talk to him. Find out, even though it had been a few weeks since he shamelessly broke up with her with a text message, if it was really what he wanted. She felt ridiculous, but at the same time it seemed right to be pursuing an answer from Harry. He wasn't like any of the others.

He's his own man, she said to herself. What was the real reason? She had to know.

She rapped again but quickly went for the hide-a-key rock and let herself in. She called out his name and flipped on some lights. The house was a mess, worse than the last time she had dropped by when Harry was ill.

Harry had come down with the flu, she remembered.

That was the last time I had seen him.

She was relieved to find his bed empty. All she needed was to walk in on Harry and another woman to feel even more removed from her usual self.

But it was close to two a.m. and Harry wasn't home nor answering his phone. She texted him: "Hey, at yr place. Worried, please get bck to me. Need to talk."

She roamed the house, looking for any clues as to where he might be. In the main bathroom, his toothbrush was still in its holder and the towels hanging on a rack were dry. His closet was full of clothes. He hadn't planned on being away long, she thought.

This is crazy, Lyndi. You've just committed a crime, breaking into his house. And now you're like a stalker trying to find out where he is.

Frustrated about what she was doing, Lyndi sat down on the couch and looked at her phone. No text back from Harry.

Something's not right.

It was that gut feeling.

She noticed a yellow legal pad of paper sitting on the coffee table, a pen next to it. The edges of the paper were ruffled and the writing on the first page looked scribbled as if by a young child. She picked it up and new from the first sentence that Harry was in trouble.

"Leroy Crump, my first client. Member of the Aryan Nation. Pure evil. Has killed and will continue to kill. I followed him once, up near Irons, Michigan. A turnoff from thirty-seven, Nine-Mile Road. You'll see a dirt road on the left that leads back into woods. That's as far as I made it. Not sure what's up that road, but bring backup. He's dangerous. I love u, LC, and I'm sorry for all this. Harry."

Lyndi quickly paged through the pad. Some sentences caught her eye: "My name is Harry Joseph West," "I went through all the stages," "Why I chose not to tell anyone."

He had told me about Crump. A skinhead.

It was all coming together now for Lyndi.

She pictured the blood smears that were left conspicuously at certain crime scenes—the images she studied for so long at the command center. Vertical and horizontal. She picked up the pen and wrote each down. When put together they formed the design of a swastika.

And the hate-crime is tied to the murders. Leroy Crump was casing his next victim when he came upon Jebediah Hatch.

But none of this mattered to her now.

Where was Harry? Does Crump have him?

She paged through more of the writings, scanning the sentences.

He was dying. He was involved. Jesus, Harry.

She gathered up the legal pad and hurried out the door.

*****

"You home yet?"

Flisk turned away from April and put his face in closer to his cellphone. "Ugh, why's that, detective?"

"I need to talk to you. It's about the murders."

Whispering now, Flisk replied, "Well, I can meet you at your place if you like? Or, the command center, of course." He sounded a little too hopeful.

"It's not like that, sergeant. I know who—" Lyndi thought about the phones. Internal investigations could be tapping into Flisk's phone. "I'll be out front of your house in two minutes."

"What? My house? How do you know where I live?"

"Who was that, D?" asked April.

"It's nothing. A detective, someone from the task force. I don't know what she wants."

April shot him a pissed-off look. "Yeah, sure."

"She's on her way over here." He sat up in bed. "She's got a lead on the case, I think. I don't know. The broad is a nut job if you ask me."

April's further inquiry was interrupted by a thumping on the front door. Flisk grabbed his handgun out of the nightstand.

"I'm scared, D," said April.

"Don't be. It wouldn't be her coming for me."

Lyndi didn't waste any time when the door opened. "I know who it is and they may have Harry West. Part of an Aryan Nation faction or something. An old client of Harry's. The leader is the perp of the hate crime in Back of the Yards. Harry may still be alive," she stopped and took a deep breath. "I'm going dark on this. I don't want to compromise anything. If I wait and this goes through the channels, Harry or someone else could end up dead. If you want in, that's up to you."

"Are you giving me a choice, detective?"

She looked at him perplexed. "Yeah, I could use the backup but I certainly don't need it."

"You're one stubborn, bitch. You know that?"

"You're either in or you're out. I don't have time for a pissing contest. I wanted to leave the information with someone in the possibility I don't make it back."

Flisk stood there, shaking his head, indicating he wasn't interested in risking his career or life for this Harry West or anyone else.

"You should go, D." April was standing in the foyer. "I know you want to."

He looked at her. "It's dangerous, April. On so many levels. And for what?"

"You're the only one she can trust." She nodded at Lyndi, who returned the gesture.

He turned back to the detective. "I have a baby girl. And a wife," he said.

"Then stay here. If you don't hear from me by sundown tomorrow, then call the super with what I've told you."

"Why don't we just call this in?"

"For personal reasons," Lyndi answered. "Listen, I'll make a deal with you: we check it out. If it's not a bust we can make alone, we'll call it in."

Flisk nodded. He turned toward April but she wasn't standing there. She had left to let them talk it over. "Well, you better tell someone else about your plans in the possibility we both don't make it out alive. I mean, detective, the Aryan Nation? Jesus, we're gonna need more firepower just in case."

"There is no one else," replied Lyndi, now growing agitated.

"Gatlin?"

"Can't be trusted."

"I don't like that prick anyway."

"I'm going now," she said and made her way to the door.

"Wait! Text me where to meet you. I think I know who will be willing to help us."

END OF THE ROAD

Autumn

Harry West was at peace

THE SMELL, RANCID and stifling, stopped Lyndi just inside the trailer's entrance. She had only moved two steps in before taking up a defensive position, crouching low with her gun, firmly gripped with both hands, out in front. The morning light, bursting behind her through the busted out door, cast a faint glow inside the trailer, but she couldn't see the entirety of the interior, only the filth in the light. She kept aim down a dark corridor where a soiled sheet hung as a curtain divider to another room.

More gunfire erupted behind her. When she went to holler over the din she tensed in pain from her wounds. Gathering her strength again, she called out, "Leroy Crump! This is the police! We have you surrounded. Put down your weapon and—"

A pasty white blob with dirty blond hair strewn across its face emerged from behind the sheet, bearing down on Lyndi on all four legs. It growled and snarled as it stomped across the trailer floor toward her.

Lyndi aimed the gun but drew back her trigger finger when she realized it was a large naked female crawling across the floor. The woman stopped, looked up menacingly at her, let go a phlegmy snarl, and drove her face into Lyndi's leg, trying to bite her.

Kicking her away, Lyndi caught the movement of the curtain again. Crump was aiming an automatic rifle at her. Instinctively, she fell to her non-wounded side, while turning the gun sideways with one hand and popping off two successive shots.

She caught a glimpse of Crump reeling back in pain and letting go a burst from the rifle before staggering forward a few steps and dropping to his knees.

The woman pounced, her weight heavy, her hands clawing at Lyndi's head and face. Lyndi tried desperately to fight her off but when she felt teeth clinch into her arm, she raised her hand and smashed the butt of the gun against the woman's head. Leveraging a foot into the woman's gut, she finally kicked her off.

The woman drew away and pushed herself up to her knees, blood trickling from her head wound, down her face. Her naked body was covered in filth and bruises. Lyndi could see the menace was now gone from her face. The growling and snarling had been replaced with deep woeful sobs.

Lyndi raised her gun. "Get the fuck out of the way!"

"I'm sorry," the woman spit as bullets from Crump's assault rifle ripped through her body in a diagonal line across her chest.

As soon as the dead woman leaned forward to fall, Lyndi pulled the trigger. The bullet hit Crump in the center of his forehead.

The two bodies hit the floor, one right after the other.

Except for the dull ringing in her ears, all went silent.

Lyndi picked herself up and staggered out of the trailer to find Jebediah and Flisk making their way toward her.

"You hit?" Flisk's voice seemed distant but she knew he was standing only a few feet away.

The murky fog was gone from the surface of the pond. The sky was a clear blue. An autumn olive fragrance languished in the air. And down by the first trailer, bodies were strewn along the dirt road.

"Is Harry here?" she asked desperately.

"No," answered Flisk. "He's not among the dead."

An image of someone standing off in the distance, holding a rifle on his shoulder, suddenly went blurry in Lyndi's eyes. She could only hope that Flisk and Jebediah both understood her words as she gestured to the road toward the vehicles.

"I've got a med kit in the trunk of my car but someone's standing …," she said before slumping down to the ground and passing out.

*****

The soreness resonated throughout her body. She knew not to move to one side, the gauze and the medical

229

tape had been administered tautly across the left side of her torso. When she looked up, Flisk was standing with his back to her, a portion of his jeans torn at the bottom revealing a leg wrapped in gauze. His neck also had a white patch with a circle of red on it.

Lyndi sat up. The sun was now high in the sky, well above the trees. "Did you call it in?"

Flisk turned around. "No," he said as he limped closer to her. "He got most of the pellets out, but I wouldn't walk through any metal detectors anytime soon if I were you."

Cautiously, Lyndi worked her way to her feet. She stood crouched over, holding her side. "Where is he?"

"The old man? He's down by the pond."

"Why?"

When Lyndi looked toward the pond she was stunned. The bodies had been laid out near the edge. Leroy Crump's and the large woman's bodies had been removed from the trailer and also dragged to the water's edge.

"What the hell's going on?" she asked.

"Well, unless you want to spend the rest of your life in a jumpsuit behind bars—"

"No, no. You gotta tell him, Flisk. This can all get sorted out. For chrise sakes, we're cops."

"Wasn't the old man's idea. It was his," Flisk pointed behind her.

Walking up the dirt road was a tall, lean, broad-shouldered man with cropped gray hair. He wore work boots, multi-pocketed dark chinos, a white long sleeve shirt and a black vest. In one hand, he held a phone which he was barking orders into. In the other hand, he dragged a body with ease by the dead man's jean jacket collar.

"Holy shit," said Lyndi with astonishment.

"Yeah, no shit," Flisk agreed. "He's been kickin our asses for the good part of an hour now."

As the man drew closer he seemed to notice Lyndi. He turned his head, nodded and grinned. "This is what happens when a woman tries to do a man's job, sweetheart," he said before passing them and continuing to bark into the phone, while still dragging the body.

With a quick motion, the man tossed the body with the others and headed back toward Lyndi and Flisk. He was soon joined by Jebediah.

"That's all of em, sir," said Jebediah.

"Good work," said the man. "I've got a military cat on the way to level these trailers and dispose of the rest of this shit hole on top of these old boys. We got enough heavy metal here, including that wrecked up Camaro, to use as anchors. We'll give these scumbags a proper burial in their own shit soon enough.

"Can't tell ya how happy I was to find we already had a hole to bury these pricks in." The man patted a shocked-looking Jebediah on the shoulder as they reached Lyndi.

"Well, Lyndi Sue, I see you went all-Wyatt Earp up here on your day off. I got most of that buckshot out of your stubborn ass, but you better promise me you're not gonna go Rambo ever again, because I've never been so goddamn busy callin in favors this mornin."

"Yes, sir," softly replied Lyndi, blinking her eyes to make sure he was real. His face was solid and cut with sharp edges. The skin was older, more wrinkled, but his eyes were as crisp as ever and he was still built like a brickhouse.

Lyndi stuttered, "How … how did you find me?"

"After you left that message, I tracked your phone through the GPS. Had a Huey chopper transport me across the lake from Great Lakes Naval Station."

Lyndi, Flisk and Jebediah seemed to stare at the man in wonder.

"Well, hell, there's no time to stand around whistlin like a couple of ferries."

"What's it been, like ten-fifteen years?" Lyndi asked.

"How about you stick a tampon in it and we finish cleanin up this mess of yours." He moved out of the small circle and began walking down the dirt road. "Now, Old Man River, Officer Gimp, and the Princess of Pistols here, we need to gather up all the weapons, every cartridge, every shell casing you can find. Rack the chambers, make sure none are loaded. Stock pile them down by the cruiser. Also, throw your personal cellphone devices in that pile. You have suddenly misplaced those items and will need to get yourself new ones. I'm going to assume that you police officers—because you don't seem like complete dumbasses—didn't use any service weapons in this here shootout. Correct?"

Lyndi and Flisk both answered simultaneously, "That's correct … sir."

He stopped suddenly and turned back to the group. "You were never here. This never happened. This place doesn't exist, not in the physical sense or in your memories. Do I make myself clear?"

He did not wait for a response. "Now stop standin around like a bunch of pansies. Let's get to work!" The man turned and started heading back down the road.

Flisk broke the silence. "We asked him who he was and all he said was, 'I'm the guy who's come to save your sorry asses.' Said if he told us his name, he'd have to kill us."

Lyndi let out a deep sigh. "His name is Jack Carnes. He's my father."

*****

She wanted to look over at him, scrutinize whether the years had made an impact on his appearance. She wanted to tell him about all the things she had accomplished since she had last seen him. She wanted to tell him about Harry West. But she knew better. They sat in silence, him driving, his eyes darting at the rearview mirrors every few minutes.

He finally spoke while they crossed the Skyway Bridge into Chicago.

"I haven't been around these parts in a long while. You got a place in mind to dump the guns and the phones? Preferably, not in an urban environment."

Lyndi took a deep breath. "Why didn't we just leave them with the rest of it?" She asked, leaning her head back against the seat and thinking about how quickly and efficiently the men her father had called had descended upon the scene. She was told to wait by the cruiser, but she lingered about, catching a glimpse of the bodies being chained to the cinder blocks that had been used as steps up to the porch of one of the trailers.

She had watched as the trailers were razed and the debris dumped into the pond by a military-grade backhoe. The pond was then filled with dirt and tree limbs.

In a manner of just thirty minutes the place had been cleared. A few trees were felled to cover the road on the way out. The backhoe was loaded onto a flatbed and covered with a black tarp. Then, the mysterious men jumped into the cab of the semitrailer and they were gone.

It was like nothing had ever existed in those woods. Lyndi had felt astonished and disturbed by how meticulous the men worked, as if the process was an acceptable routine.

"Because you don't want to leave everything in one place," answered her father. "And, besides, it's not right to bury perfectly good firearms with shitbags like that. I'd call it sacrilegious as a matter of fact. "

The emotion came with a rush of pain. Her wounds ached. Beyond tired now, her mind wasn't at its strongest.

It was the first time Lyndi Carnes had cried for as long as she could remember. The last time may have been when her father didn't return from his mission. And now there she was sitting right next to him, weeping like a child. She wanted to say to him, "So much death. It's too much to bear." But, instead, she gathered herself and sat up.

"Can you do me one more favor?" she asked in a hardy voice.

Her father looked at her sternly. "Sure, Lyndi Sue. What is it?"

"Find a friend of mine, Harry West. He's likely dead."

The stern look melted away. "You know, sometimes some men just don't want to be found, dead or alive."

They sat in silence for a few minutes, Lyndi angrily wiping away any tears.

"I'll see what I can do," he said, patting her leg.

"I know a place," she said assertively. "We can bypass the city. It's about sixty miles west."

*****

He handed her a black overcoat. "Here, your jackets got rat holes in it. Use this." He turned and looked around. What is this place anyway?"

She slipped on the coat and carefully started to walk the bank of the crick, toward the clump of forest well beyond the farmhouse.

"You sure you don't want me to do this and you wait in the car?" he asked.

She turned back to him. "Follow me," she said, throwing at her father his own steely glare.

He picked up the large duffle bags of guns and did what he was told.

Before entering the forest, she stopped and looked up at the trees. A breeze ruffled the leaves, their orange and red colors fusing with the golden hue of dusk. She felt something. She clutched her side and hurried into the woods.

Nearly slipping down the slope to the pond, she saw his body laid out near the water's edge. She hurried down to him as best she could, her wounds aching with each step.

There on the landing she kneeled down and touched his arm. She heard her father's footsteps come up behind her.

"More shitbags? Jeezus, Lyndi Sue, did you kill this guy, too?"

Lyndi covered her eyes. She didn't want her father to see her cry again. She felt his hand on her shoulder.

"I'll go find something to dig with in the shed by the farmhouse," he said softly to her. She touched his hand and looked up at him. "Stay frosty," he told her.

"He was good man," she said.

Jack Carnes nodded and slowly moved away.

Lyndi turned back to Harry. He had died with his eyes open. She had seen this from the dead before and it was always unnerving. But for some reason Harry looked content. He had been looking directly up.

She turned her head toward the sky and took in the canvass of leaves above them. It brought her some relief knowing the colors were the last thing he had seen before he died.

Harry West was at peace.

*****

"You're in no shape to go home, and, besides, you shouldn't let your wife and daughter see you this way," Jebediah raised his hand to stop Flisk from objecting. "Nope—"

"They went to April's mom's place last night as soon as I left," said Flisk.

"Well, you're in no shape to be sittin alone. You can stay at my place a couple days till your back on your feet. I got a landline, see. You can call her, tell her you're okay. Old people still believe in landlines."

"Well, I'm gonna need to call the station and tell them I'm out ill for a while." Flisk moved his tender neck to look at the old man. "You really want me to stay in the hood with you?"

They both grinned.

"You scared?" Jebediah's mouth stretched into a smile. "As good a place as any, I suppose," he said while turning the car onto Forty-seventh Street, the late afternoon sun glaring off the windshield.

"You been thinking about it at all, during the drive?" asked Flisk.

"Bout killin those fellas?"

"Nah, about how you walked through a hail of bullets unscathed?"

They both began to laugh.

"Yeah, that was a blessed miracle," said Jebediah, pulling the car off Forty-seventh into an alley and then into his garage. "I think I need to thank the good Lord for watchin over me on that one."

As he helped Flisk out of the car and the two made their way inside his home, Jebediah felt the shock of the morning's shootout and aftermath begin to wear off. He was pleased that Flisk was going to stick around a day or two. It would help keep his mind off of everything.

"I'll fry us up something to eat." He helped Flisk into the living room and down onto the old sofa. Dusk was settling outside and the room was dark.

"You know how to make a grilled cheese sandwich?" asked Flisk.

When Jebediah went to turn on the lamp, he noticed the man sitting in his barcalounger, holding a gun on his lap, a duffel bag at his feet.

"Sit down, *viejo*."

"Who's tellin me to sit down in my own home?" Jebediah barked.

The man reached over to the lamp and tugged the pull-chain.

When the light revealed who was sitting in the chair, Jebediah tensed and instinctively reached for his Kimber. "What the hell you think you're doing in my house?" When he realized the gun wasn't there he relaxed and took a deep breath. "How'd you get in here?"

"Sit down," Raymond Delgado repeated, pointing with his gun to the chair behind the old man, and watching him step back and slowly lower himself.

"You do anything stupid here and you better have a secret tunnel from here to Mexico," said Flisk, his face turning pale.

"You come to kill us, boy? Because as you can see," Jebediah gestured toward Flisk, "someone may have already tried that on us today and it didn't work out too good for them."

"You've a nice *casa*, *viejo*. You raise *las hijas* here?" Delgado nodded at his own question while peering up at the framed photographs on the mantel. "Nice *familia*. Me, no *familia*. Me *madre* a whore. Me *padre* a drug addict."

"And you a cockroach drug dealer is what you are," said Jebediah.

"I'm not a cockroach." Delgado paused and Jebediah could see tears well up in his eyes. "*Soy sobreviviente*." He moved the gun from his lap and put it on the end table next to the chair. "I am a survivor."

In a low, desperate voice, Jebediah asked, "Raymond, what are you doing here?"

Delgado adjusted in his seat and cleared his throat. "I come across the border a young pisser tuggin on my mother's arm. She towing five others, three of us only make it. Two died of disease. One is a junkie begger in Juarez. I hopped around from uncle to aunt for a while. But then I flunked out of school before I could get kicked out. I had nobody to help me or nobody cared enough to force me to go.

"Tried to work as a laborer but I needed more than that, ya know. You can't get more than that without school. The gang come around and swept me up. First time I ever felt I had a purpose. First time I ever felt a real sense of *familia*.

"When I was thirteen, I beat up some kid for mouthin off about our gang and, man, everything went *loco* from there. I was put on a pedestal. I was *el rey del mundo*, the king of the world.

"But I've done some bad things since that first punch." Delgado looked over at Flisk. "I've killed. Now some, some *vatos* had it comin." He swallowed hard. "Some didn't. There's an Asian fella in a wheelchair cuz of me. Was at a mall once, scopin *cholas*, and swear to god I see the guy. He's wheelin 'round, and I tell my homies the story and laugh at him. And then this little *chico* walks up to him and jumps up in his lap, and the guy just wheels himself off with the kid smiling."

Delgado put his hand over his eyes. Jebediah caught a glance from Flisk but shook him off, even raising his hand. "How old are you, Raymond?" he asked.

"I am probably twenty-eight or twenty-nine." He took a deep breath.

"Why don't you get yourself out? Move away, start over," said Flisk.

Raymond shot a look at him, "How's that working out for you, homie?"

Jebediah spoke up. "You could disappear, blend in. What's the harm in that?"

"It aint that simple, *viejo*. The Kings are run by a much higher power in Mexico. There is no disappearing from the cartel unless the cartel wants you to disappear. And they are here," he pointed at the floor. "Right here in Chicago.

"You know that boy that got shot? They snuck in a young *asesino* from Mexico for that. Killed a gangbanger's kid, a little *chico*, just to make a statement. That *familia* beat and cut in Gage Park? Los Zetas trying to make claim to more turf. That's how ruthless it is now. It's a different ballgame round here than it was."

Jebediah fidgeted nervously. "What do you want from us?" he asked.

"I wanted to say that I'm sorry for not helping you in the street that night. It was wrong. And for everything I done and said to you. And I'm just sorry for everything. If you need anything—"

"I won't take a damn thing from no gangbanger," said Jebediah.

"That's just it, *viejo*. I aint gonna be no gangbanger no more. I'm done. I was gonna go back to Guanajuato and try to live quietly, but that's a pipe dream.

"No, I aint leavin the Yards. I have some money that my enemies did not find." Delgado gestured toward the duffel bag on the floor. "Two hundred seventy-seven K. All in cash. I want it to go to the neighborhood. I want you to see to it that it's used for good things. Hell, maybe some of the tykes down on Wolcott can use it to get an education or somethin. Or maybe you can use it to build a park in the vacant lot. Maybe a library or a youth center. You know, somethin nice."

"Why don't you give them your drug money yerself," said Jebediah, defiantly.

"They'll take it if it's from you," Delgado leaned forward, on the brink of tears again. "I've done some bad things in my life. And maybe this will help with whatever's to come for me." He took a deep breath and turned his attention to Flisk. "I'll give you all I know about the cartel as long as it's just between the two of us and no one else is brought in." He paused for a moment. "You help me get out, and I'll help you bag the head of the Sinaloas."

An awkward silence filled the room as Flisk stared at Delgado.

Jebediah felt the need to speak up. "Believe me, son, there are bad people everywhere in this world. All kinds."

Delgado looked at him incredulously. "I had to kill two of my closest and most loyal brothers." He took a deep breathe. "Because they were bad men."

Jebediah swallowed hard and spoke in a low voice. "Well, we know a little somethin about killing now ourselves. And what you're doing is making an effort to change, and the Bible say penitence goes a long way in God's eyes. Aint that right, Flisk?"

"Amen," Flisk replied.

The three men shared a grin.

Jebediah stood up. "As a neighbor of mine, you are my friend." He took a step forward and held out his hand. "Nice to meet you, Mr. Delgado. The name's Jebediah Hatch."

Raymond Delgado stood up and shook Jebediah's hand. He then turned to Flisk.

"Well, this is gonna be interesting," said Flisk, returning the handshake.

"Yes, it will, *amigo*," replied Delgado.

"I got a few cold ones in the ice box," mumbled Jebediah as he began to make his way from the room.

Delgado stopped him by asking a profound question. "Do you think peace will ever come to this city?"

Jebediah turned around. After a long, silent pause, he looked intently at both men. "Yes, I do," he answered. "Down the road. Down the road."

www.ingramcontent.com/pod-product-compliance
Lightning Source LLC
Chambersburg PA
CBHW060314260626
47160CB00007B/2605